RAKEHELL'S DAUGHTER

In a remote part of Cornwall Jacey Trevallion waits impatiently for the opportunity to go to London for the Season, whilst her father, Sir John, leads a dissipated life in Society heedless of the needs of his lovely and spirited daughter.

When the summons finally arrives Jacey is overjoyed, but her delight soon evaporates on her arrival to discover her father so much in debt he has been obliged to pledge her entailed dowry to the equally dissolute Earl of Sheringham.

To save Sir John from imprisonment in a debtor's jail, Jacey agrees to marry the earl, but immediately vows to try and effect a match between her father and the immensely wealthy Marchioness of Moncourt, which would enable Sir John to pay off all his debts.

Jacey's first meeting with her future husband is an unfortunate one and, unable to hide her dislike of him, she becomes even more determined to effect a match between Lady Moncourt and Sir John, but when the plan succeeds Jacey discovers what her true feelings are at last. It seems that she is not so averse to the earl after all.

RAKEHELL'S DAUGHTER

Rachelle Edwards

ROBERT HALE · LONDON

© Rachelle Edwards 1982
First published in Great Britain 1982

ISBN 0 7091 9743 8;

Robert Hale Limited
Clerkenwell House
Clerkenwell Green
London EC1R 0HT

Photoset in North Wales by
Derek Doyle & Associates, Mold, Clwyd
Printed in Great Britain by
St. Edmundsbury Press, Bury St. Edmunds, Suffolk.
Bound by Hunter & Foulis Limited

One

Trevallion Cove was but a small indentation in the coast of Cornwall, barely discernible on all but the most detailed maps. Elevated from the sea, an Elizabethan Manor stood sentinel over the coast.

For generations brave seamen of the Trevallion family had served a succession of sovereigns and had been handsomely rewarded for their valour, but that was no more. The present inhabitant, Sir John Trevallion, served his sovereign only by a token of loyalty to the Crown. His pleasure was to be found in the gambling salons of the *ton*, and in a great many other less salubrious establishments.

Sir John was a rare visitor to his family seat since the death of his wife fifteen years earlier, and the house was beginning to show signs of neglect.

As the gulls wheeled noisily overhead, a solitary figure walked along the water's edge in the shadow of the house. Her head of golden curls was bowed, the hem of her white muslin gown stained by a mixture of sand and salt water.

She walked along totally unobserved, as she had in years past. If, as rumour had it, smugglers used the many Cornish coves to land their illicit cargoes, none had ever been seen at Trevallion, much to the girl's disappointment.

As she walked, she appeared to be studying the sand into which her slippered feet sank. Every now and again she would look up and study the horizon, and occasionally she would venture a step or two further into the water which gently creamed against the rocks at the water's edge. All was calm now, but she had often witnessed those cruel and ferocious storms which lit up the horizon, and it was those occasions that she enjoyed the most.

Suddenly her head jerked up at the sound of an intrusive noise. The water welled up around her ankles although at that moment she was unaware of it, for one of the servants was running across the lawns towards her.

"Miss Jacey! Oh, Miss Jacey, so there you are!"

The girl, suddenly aware of her wet feet, lifted her skirt free of the water and, choking back a cry of exasperation at having her idyll interrupted, went forward to meet the maidservant.

"What on earth is the trouble, Betsey? Is the house burning down? Has Baines been bitten by a goat again?"

"Beggin' your pardon, ma'am, but Miss Trevallion is asking for you. In a fair old pucker she is."

"When she is not I shall have true cause for alarm," the girl replied, laughing at last.

"Well you might scoff, ma'am, but if you don't come right away I'll be bound to burn feathers. She is in such a takin'."

"Very well; I'll come in. No doubt it is a crisis of magnificent proportions, like the butcher failing to hang the meat for long enough, or, heaven forbid, forgetting to deliver it at all." She cast the maid a mischievous grin. "Where is my aunt to be found?"

"In the parlour, ma'am. At least she was a few minutes ago." The maidservant glanced askance at Jacey's bare arms. "Just as well you do come in now, ma'am; you'll catch your death out here for sure."

"Oh, the weather is glorious just now and not like to last. You mustn't scold me, Betsey. 'Tis enough my Aunt Trevallion is constantly in a fidge over my health. If I did contract fever it would at least provide us all with a diversion. Life is deadly dull here."

The maid looked shocked. "Miss Trevallion! You mustn't tempt fate so. 'Tis wicked, it is."

Jacey laughed which startled a flock of birds out of the trees. "You must own, Betsey, it would be most diverting for something to happen. Nothing ever does."

"You should be glad of that, ma'am."

"One of my ancestors was kidnapped from her bed in this very house one hundred and fifty years ago. She was carried off to sea by a buccaneer on the very eve of her wedding to a man chosen by her father."

Betsey eyed her wryly. "Aye, and she died on some heathen isle of the fever not long afterwards."

Jacey skipped across the grass. "A short life but a happy one, Betsey. I'll warrant she was not bored."

She ran through the old knot garden, now neglected and overgrown, lifting her skirt free of the path. The window to the downstairs parlour was as usual unlocked and she slipped inside. Surprisingly there was no sign of her aunt. There was, however, an empty glass on the oak table and lifting it gingerly Jacey sniffed at it. As she put it down again she recognised the smell of porter and knew her aunt could not be too far away.

A moment later the door opened and as Jacey turned around her aunt came in. Her thin features relaxed a little as she clapped eyes on her niece.

"Ah, so there you are. We have been scouring the house for you. Where have you..." Her gaze travelled downwards and her jaw gaped. "Oh, really, Jacey, you have been walking in the sea again. The hem of your gown is caked with sand. The stains of sea water will never come out."

"It is of no account, Aunt. There is no one but us to see and remark upon the disgraceful state of my clothing."

Miss Trevallion shook her head sadly. "What am I to do with you? Your disregard of your clothing is one thing, but if you persist in dipping your feet in sea water you will be certain to catch you death, and what will your father say then, I wonder?"

"He will heartily regret his neglect of me," Jacey answered impishly. "In any event, I believe it is quite fashionable to be dipped in the sea. Even the King himself has been dipped."

"So it is said although I for one cannot credit it, and if it is so 'tis no wonder the poor man ails so."

Her aunt, clad in brown bombazine, a lace cap primly on her greying hair, looked more put-upon than usual.

"There are times when I feel the guardianship of a young girl is too much for me. If only your Mama had lived ..."

"Oh, indeed, Aunt Minerva; I own it was exceeding inconsiderate of her to die."

Miss Trevallion cast her niece an exasperated look. "All I meant to say was that she was the only person who ever had any control over your father. A scapegrace he was, and always will be, I fear."

Her niece merely looked amused. It always amazed

her that this ascerbic spinster and her handsome devil-may-care father were related at all, let alone brother and sister. It was to Jacey the most amazing quirk of nature.

"I quite agree with you, Aunt. You should not be called upon to bear my hoydenish ways. I know how it oversets your nerves. You must tell Papa so, and as soon as possible. He must be made to take responsibility for me."

Her aunt cast her a disbelieving look. "As ever you are roasting me. If I give you a set-down it is purely for your own well-being."

"Yes, Aunt," Jacey replied with mock humility, "but I beg of you not to scold me for doing my patriotic duty to King and country."

Her aunt continued to look irritated. "What humbug is this? What is patriotic about wading into treacherous water?"

Jacey was wide-eyed. "I spend my time at the sea-shore in order to espy any enemy invasion the moment it occurs. You know full well, Aunt, it is incumbent upon all of us to watch for the arrival of Bonaparte so that an alarm can be raised at the earliest possible moment."

The colour seemed to drain from her aunt's cheeks and she gripped a china cabinet for support. "Bonaparte. Oh, Jacey, do you really think that monster will come?"

"It has been generally held that an invasion has been imminent for months. If he does come it is like to be before the winter sets in."

"Oh, dear. Oh dear, oh dear!"

Minerva Trevallion hurried to the settle and eased herself into it. "It hardly bears contemplating."

Immediately regretful, Jacey said in a soothing tone, "Well, it is not certain that he will come, so you must not fret, but I own it would be quite diverting if he did."

Her aunt looked horrified. "Oh, you wicked, wicked girl! Diverting indeed! How can you say so?"

"The monotony is quite wearing. If the Corsican Upstart comes he is sure to bring others with him. There may even be balls and routs held by them for the local gentry."

Minerva Trevallion's hand clenched into a fist. "We are more like to have our throats cut – or worse."

"Worse?" Jacey asked in all innocence. "What, pray, can be worse than having one's throat cut?"

When her aunt did not answer Jacey poured out a glass of porter and handed it to her. "Don't get into a pucker, Aunt. I am persuaded it will not happen, and if it does it will be in Kent or Sussex, or perhaps even Scotland. They would not dare invade England at Trevallion's Cove." Then she added, "It would not accommodate their boats."

Minerva Trevallion took the proferred glass. "You are for ever gammoning me. Shall you take nothing to heart?"

Jacey went to sit in one of the Windsor chairs near the fireplace, clasping her hands in her lap in a more demure manner than she usually adopted.

"Betsey said you wanted to see me. She was in quite a pucker so I trust there is not a crisis."

"So do I," her aunt replied in heartfelt tones, putting down the empty glass. "Indeed I do."

For the first time Jacey noticed that her aunt was clasping a sheet of parchment to her bosom. Her heart quickened as she recognised the broken seal.

"You have heard from Papa!"

Miss Trevallion sighed. "Indeed."

Jacey's eyes grew bright. "Oh, do tell me what he says! Is he coming home, Aunt Minerva? Do say he is on his way to Cornwall. I'm in a fidge to know."

"He is not returning at present," As Jacey's countenance fell she added, "Which is very foolish of him. There are a great many matters here which need his attention, not the least of them a growing girl."

"I am already fully grown, Aunt."

"Well, he should certainly attend his estate rather than leave it to that rascally Didcome, whom I swear robs him at every turn. If our pockets are to let it is only –"

Jacey had heard it all before and broke in impatiently, "Yes, indeed, Aunt, but what does Papa *say*? I know of old he would not write unless he had *something* to impart."

It seemed that Aunt Minerva's lips looked a mite more pinched and disapproving than was usual.

"You are correct, my dear. Your father wishes us to join him in London as soon as it is possible."

The words were scarcely out of her aunt's lips when Jacey jumped to her feet. She danced around the room in delight.

"London! I can scarce believe I am actually to go to London at last. Oh, Aunt Minerva, my prayers are answered. I have prayed for this for so long."

"Shame on you for troubling the Lord on so trivial a matter."

Jacey, however, was not set-down. She continued to dance around the room. "I am to have a Season after all. I shall be presented to the Queen, and the Prince of Wales! I can scarcely contain my delight! It will be so wonderful. London! A Season! Just imagine it, Aunt Minerva."

"That is precisely what I am doing, but I would not rely upon that being your father's reason for sending for us, dear. He makes no mention of it in his letter."

"That is of no account. Why else would he wish me to join him? In London." Her eyes grew bright again. "I can scarce wait to attend all those balls and routs, the theatre, Vauxhall Gardens. Oh, Aunt Minerva, it will be sublime."

"I do hope you are correct, but it is more like your father has some scheme afoot. I should think he is too far in dun territory to be spending the blunt on launching you."

"Tush, Aunt Minerva," Jacey scolded, but not unkindly. Her aunt's habitual pessimism was no stranger to her. "There can only be one reason for his wishing us to go. You really must credit Papa for some goodness. He is not so bad as you make out,"

"My dear, he is not bad at all – merely foolish. He was ever foolish. He was always a wild youth and since your dear Mama's untimely death has reverted to his rakehell ways with a vengeance. I dread to imagine how he passes his time in Town."

Jacey chuckled. "Why, Aunt Minerva, no doubt he is having a cracking time."

Miss Trevallion made a sound of derision. "To his mind, perchance, but I cannot conceive that coming out in his company will bode anything but ill for you."

Jacey was already making for the door. "I refuse to listen to such megrims, Aunt Minerva. You may be Friday-faced if you please but I am going to instruct my maid to pack immediately."

"That will not take too long, I fancy."

The girl smiled again as she paused by the door. "No, indeed. I have not the least intention of taking my old dowdy clothes to London. I shall take only the essentials, for Papa is sure to insist upon clothing me anew from head to foot when I arrive."

The door closed with a loud bang behind her and Miss Trevallion was left to shake her head whilst her niece fled upstairs, calling excitedly for her maid.

Two

Even though Sir John Trevallion's travelling carriage was not the most stylish or comfortable, Jacey enjoyed every minute of her ride to London, mainly because her mind dwelled constantly on the delights which surely awaited her at journey's end.

There had been a delay which vexed her. Her aunt, who was unused to the rigours of travelling, felt sufficiently indisposed to insist upon remaining an extra night at one of the inns at which they were obliged to put up, leaving Jacey to wait impatiently for the resumption of their journey.

There were times when the carriage became unbearably hot because Miss Trevallion would not countenance the window to be open, even a little, but such bagatelles could not dampen Jacey's enthusiasm.

Her eyes opened wide when the last of the countryside was left behind and the carriage began to pass through the streets of London. Jacey had never seen so many people who thronged the narrow walks which edged the road. Milkmaids and pedlars mingled with beggars and elegantly dressed dandies.

The roads, too, were thronged with an odd assortment of vehicles. Vendors carts struggled along whilst smart phaetons and gigs streaked past them, often avoiding a collision by a hair's breadth. Pedestrians seemed not to heed the wheeled traffic at all and when coachmen were obliged to call out a warning as they bore down on people, a good deal of bad-tempered cursing was the result on all sides.

The air was filled with a cacophony of new sounds, so strange after the peace of Cornwall. Pedlars called out their wares, pedestrians cursed the carriages which sprayed mud on them as they sped by, and the noise of wheels and hooves was like thunder itself.

Jacey peered out of the carriage window wide-eyed, even though they were not making as much progress as she would have wished. The previous night had been a sleepless one, so excited was she at the prospect of being in London and seeing her father again. She wasn't certain which was the brighter prospect; a combination of the two was perfection.

"Oh, do put your head inside," her aunt urged, "or you are like to have it knocked off your shoulders, not to mention the danger of a draught on me."

"But there is so much to see! So much colour and life. In my dreams I never imagined it to be so exciting. Oh, over there! Sir, oh, sir, do beware!"

She had caught sight of a cut-purse making off with a gentleman's money. She shouted out her warning, laughing delightedly when the robber's victim set off down an alley in pursuit. Then she sank back into the squabs, still laughing.

"Babel," her aunt murmured, closing her eyes. "I knew it would be Babel. How can anyone bear it? I declare I shall not."

Reluctantly Jacey drew her attention away from the

sights and sounds of the capital. "It is wonderful," she breathed. "I have actually seen people wearing clothes that I have only seen in fashion plates. I cannot wait to visit the shops and emporiums, Aunt Minerva."

"For that one needs funds, Jacey. We have none, you will recall. Whenever we are in funds – and that is rare enough – your father games it away with little delay."

"He may have won a fortune this time for all we know."

"If he had, he will have lost it by now, you may be certain."

Jacey put one hand over her aunt's as the woman winced. The carriage had jolted badly over a pot-hole, of which there seemed to be a great many.

"Dear Aunt Minerva, must you be so Friday-faced? We are here in London and we are going to be with Papa again. That is the greatest pleasure. In any event I shall be happy enough just to look at the goods on view in the shops. One needs no money to look."

"That is not my experience of this town."

Jacey looked at her with interest. "What is your experience, Aunt Minerva?"

"Not a happy one, I fear. I was once your age, although you may take leave to doubt it now. I came to London to make my debut ..."

"I didn't know! Oh, Aunt Minerva, how wonderful for you! Do tell me all about it."

Her thin lips curved into a bitter smile. "I was even about to become betrothed during that Season. However," she added with a sigh, "your Grandfather Trevallion, had gambled away my portion."

Jacey's hold on her aunt's hand tightened and her

bright demeanour gave way to dismay. "Poor Aunt
Minerva, I didn't know. I am so sorry."

"There has never been anything to gain by
discussing it. The sadness was only a fleeting one."
She cast a smile at her niece. "I have been happy at
Trevallion Manor, you need not doubt. He could not
have lived without a portion from his bride. It was a
matter of necessity, as with so many men. I bear him
no malice, for I understood all too well, and on
reflection I believe I had a fortunate escape from what
might have been an unhappy marriage."

Jacey could not envisage her aunt ever being young
or inviting the attention of a gentleman. She did pause
to wonder what manner of a woman her aunt might
have been if fate had decreed her to be fulfilled by
marriage.

"At least that cannot happen to me," she mused, for
once her spirits a little dampened. "Grandfather
Dayton ensured that Papa could not touch my
portion."

Minerva Trevallion gave one of her rare laughs.
"He was indeed a wise man. Of course he knew your
father for what he undoubtedly is. A rakehell of the
first order. Lord Dayton never approved of that
marriage and although he could do nothing to save the
dissipation of your Mama's portion he could certainly
provide you with one which might not be touched."

Jacey sank back into the creaking squabs. "I am
delighted they proved him wrong about one matter;
Mama and Papa were madly in love and terribly
happy. I only hope I find a man like Papa who wishes
to marry me."

Her aunt gasped. "And I pray most fervently that
you do not."

"I assure you I have no mind to be wed for my portion."

"There is little chance you will be wed without one, my girl."

"Then I would be glad enough to remain a spinster and return to Cornwall for ever."

Miss Trevallion smiled again. "That has suited me well enough, but I fear it will not do for you."

"I dare say it will not have to, for I do have my portion and I'd as lief wed a penniless rake as some worthy bore with a hundred properties."

The carriage came to a halt outside a neat terrace overlooking a square.

"We are arrived!" Jacey exclaimed, sitting forward again.

"The Lord be praised! I am all done up. Travelling, I declare, is an invention of the Devil."

Jacey wasted no time in climbing down, eagerly glancing around. "So this is Bloomsbury," she breathed, shivering with excitement.

Then, recalling her aunt, she turned to give her an arm as she waved away the footman who would have come to her aid.

"I wonder if Papa is in, waiting for us," Jacey ventured as they passed into the narrow hall.

"At this time? I take leave to doubt it. Take my advice, child, and reconcile yourself to not seeing him before noon tomorrow. Ah, Betsey, there you are," she greeted her maid who came hurrying from the back of the house. "I am all done up. The journey was atrocious. I have never been so jolted in my life."

"We were not held up by a tobyman," Jacey pointed out in a bright tone which only elicited a groan from her aunt.

"Never you mind, ma'am," crooned the maid, taking hold of her mistress's arm. "There's a brick in your bed and a posset on the boil. You'll soon feel much better, you'll see."

Jacey drew a sigh of relief as Betsey took charge of her aunt and led her towards the stairs. She removed her bonnet and handed it together with her gloves to the house-steward.

"Welcome to Trevallion House, madam. All is in readiness for your arrival in accordance with Sir John's instructions."

Jacey cast him an absent smile as she continued to glance around. At least in her father's town house there was little sign of neglect. There was also little sign of affluence, too, but Jacey had not expected to find any.

"Thank you, er ...?"

"Cranford, madam."

"When will Sir John be home, Cranford?"

"He has not gone out today, madam."

At last he had Jacey's full attention. Her eyes opened wide. "Sir John is actually here in the house?"

"Yes, madam."

"That is indeed splendid news! I trust he will receive me with no further delay."

"As to that I cannot say, madam. Sir John is unfortunately indisposed today and confined to his bed. We are just now awaiting the arrival of the physician."

Her bright countenance faded to be replaced by a look of alarm. "Sir John is ill? I cannot credit this."

"I regret that it is so, madam."

"Is it serious?" Her voice was now no more than a whisper.

"That I cannot say, madam. His valet, Simpson, was sufficiently concerned to send for a physician."

Jacey's trembling hands flew to her lips. "Oh, my goodness. I must go to him immediately."

She started towards the stairs and the house-steward said, "It would be best if you were to await Sir John's instructions, madam."

"He will want to see me. Which is his room? Come Cranford, do not delay."

The man sighed. "Very well, madam. Follow me."

He led the way up the stairs and Jacey could scarce conceal her anxiety or her concern whilst Cranford tapped at the door. Her father's valet admitted her to the darkened room which was lit only by the glow of the fire and a solitary candle. The constant noise of traffic in the square below was muffled by the heavy curtains which had been drawn across the windows.

With scarce a nod to the valet Jacey hurried to the bed, her heart full of trepidation for what she might find. The curtains had been partially closed around the bed and the valet pulled one aside so that she could see her father. The sight of him gave her a shock, for he seemed to have shrunk. His normally animated face was drawn and ashen, his chin furred with two or three days' growth of beard.

"He has been asleep for some time," the servant told her. "I beg of you not to disturb him, madam."

"I shall be most circumspect." Without taking her eyes from her father's inert form she asked then, with a slight hesitation, "How ill is he?"

"I cannot say, madam."

"Then tell me how long he has been like this?" she insisted.

"He was suddenly afflicted. Yesterday he was in

high snuff, as always, madam. In truth I cannot understand it."

Her entire body was then afflicted with dread and she sank down into a chair at the bedside, every limb trembling.

"I do not suppose you know what it is that afflicts him so sorely?"

"No, madam. I regret I do not. You may as well leave him to me," he told her gently after a moment's pause. "I shall not leave him and there is nought you can do."

"Oh no, I shall stay. I would want to be here when he awakes."

"Very well, madam, if that is what you wish."

Unwillingly she drew her gaze away from her father's face and looked at the valet at last. "If you would like to rest whilst I remain here you may do so. I shall not leave him."

"Thank you, madam. I shall take refreshment and then return as soon as the physician arrives."

As the door clicked shut behind him Jacey looked at Sir John once more, tears pricking at her eyes.

"Dear Papa," she whispered, "I pray that this is not the end of our reunion."

There was not a time she could recall him being other than in the rudest health, and the greatest spirits. Trevallion Manor was an empty shell during his frequent absences, but when he was in residence the ancient walls resounded with the sound of his laughter. Jacey did not wonder that her mother had married him in spite of her family's disapproval.

Long dark eyelashes so like her own fanned out on his cheeks and a fair curl had fallen across his brow. Unable to resist the gesture Jacey leaned forward and gently brushed it away.

He stirred then and she froze in her seat. "Who is that? Simpson? Simpson, is that you?"

"No, Papa. 'Tis I, your daughter."

"Jacey. Jacey here in London? Why? Why are you here?"

His voice was no more than a whisper but eagerly she answered, "You sent for me. Do you not recall?"

A deep sigh seemed to escape his body. "Yes, yes, I recall now." His eyelids fluttered open. "Jacey, my dear, dear girl. I dreamed you would come. I knew you would be here. You would never fail me, would you?"

She smiled down at him. "No, Papa, I would never do that. I shall not leave you now. How do you feel?"

"A little better, but confoundedly weak."

Anxiously she asked, "Are you in pain?"

"Not any longer. Simpson gave me laudanum. Now only my head hurts. Your presence can only result in an improvement, I fancy." His hand sought out hers which he grasped in a surprisingly firm way. He smiled faintly. "My little Jacey. You are all grown up and so beautiful."

Her throat was so tight with emotion she could hardly speak. "You must not talk, Papa. You must rest as much as you can."

"There is very little else I can do. I am as weak as a babe."

"It will soon be better."

"Is ... Minerva with you?"

"Of course."

"Don't ... allow her in here I beg of you."

"She will insist upon it, Papa, once she knows you are ill."

"Then delay in telling her. It would be an act of mercy." She smiled faintly as he added, "Her ministrations would be too much just now. No strength to withstand her set-downs ..."

Jacey managed a smile again as his voice faded away, "You need not fear. She is all done up after the journey and it is like she will remain in her room at least four and twenty hours."

"That is a mercy. I ... hoped she would stay at Trevallion. I fear m'sister hasn't changed. Tongue doused in vinegar."

For a few moments it seemed as though he had fallen asleep once more. Jacey wished the physician would hurry as she was desperately worried. Only an illness of considerable severity would cause him to take to his bed.

Suddenly Sir John's grip on her hand tightened once again. "Jacey."

"I am still here, Papa."

His eyes seemed to be filled with pain. "I have something to tell you – before it is too late."

"Too late," she echoed in dismay. A hand of dread squeezed at her heart. "Do not speak in such a manner, I beg of you."

"Too late to mince words, my lovely. 'Tis of the greatest import what I have to say, and we must face up to the inevitable."

Once again tears pricked at her eyes. "Oh, Papa, I beg of you do not say so."

"Listen, listen to what I have to say. It is time you were wed ..."

"Yes, yes, of course. When you are well again ..."

"No time, I fear, so I have made arrangements..."

"Let us wait until you are well again," she answered, laughing uncertainly.

"No! There is not time to wait and I must ... tell ... you ..."

His voice faded again and she bit her lip. "Yes, Papa?"

When he didn't speak or move for a few minutes she began to panic. Then to her profound relief he began to stir again.

"Jacey, you must allow me to know what is right for you."

"I do," she assured him.

She was convinced he did not know what he was saying. In fact she feared he did not truly know she was there.

"I have arranged a marriage for you."

From the depths of her despair Jacey was now staggered at his statement. Her blue eyes opened wide with shock.

"Papa!"

"Oh, I know you will be surprised, but it is a good match. The Earl of Sheringham. I know him well."

"Papa," she whispered in bewilderment, "why? Why have you felt the need to provide me with a husband?"

"'Tis a parent's solemn duty to do so."

Still bewildered she whispered, afraid of causing him distress, "You never used to be so old-fashioned."

"It is my dearest wish to see you ... settled before ... I ..."

"Don't say it! You are not going to die and when I marry it will be to a man of my own choosing and you will be there to witness it."

"If only that could be, but it is all arranged. You must not gainsay me, Jacey. There is little time, I fear."

He seemed at that moment to collapse into unconsciousness once more and she brushed away the tears from her cheeks.

"Papa," she begged, "you cannot truly wish me to do this. 'Tis a fever, that is all. You cannot know what you are asking of me."

"I fear I must tell you the truth," he gasped and the ghost of a smile crossed his face. "You were always too sharp to be a cully. It was ... unfair of me to try."

"Then ... it is not true after all? You were gammoning me, Papa."

"If only that were so. Truth to tell, my lovely, your Papa is in the devil of a fix. Sheringham is dunning me."

Once more Jacey went stiff with shock. "For how much?"

"I owe him a fortune, don't you see? Your portion is the only way out of this morass."

"Surely not?"

She put one hand to her aching head. It was all too much for her to bear in one afternoon. His illness, an arranged marriage, now a hint of dire trouble.

"Would you have me spend what is left of my life in the Fleet?"

Jacey withdrew from him at last. "So that is the way of it. How could you become inveigled in this mess, Papa?"

He shook his head back and forth in distress. "I beg of you do not scold me. I am despicable, I know it. I am paying the price as you can see, but there is little time left. 'Tis all agreed. You must give me your word, Jacey. You will marry Sheringham. He is not a bad fellow."

"Not bad! Threatening you with the Fleet!"

"He is entitled to his money. He has been patient enough until now."

"Is he in agreement?"

"Naturally. Your portion is not inconsiderable."

She turned away from him in distress. "There must be another way."

"Oh, I have tried, and only sunk deeper into the mire. If there was any other way, believe me ..."

"He must be a monster," she cried in outraged tones.

"You mustn't blame Sheringham. I am a foolish gamester, for ever believing Lady Luck will favour me. You portion will cover what he is owed handsomely. The only way ... forgive me ..."

Tears began to flow down her cheeks once more as she held his hand up to her face. "Of course I forgive you, Papa."

"And you will ... marry Sheringham? Give me your word, Jacey, whilst I am still able to hear it."

Choking back her tears she answered, "You have my word, Papa. I will not be the cause of your disgrace."

He sighed and sank back into the pillows. "You deserve better than to be used in this way, but what else is left to me except disgrace? Don't think I care for myself, for I do not, but I have a heed for the name of Trevallion." He laughed brokenly. "I know I have disappointed you."

"No, no, you must not think so. After all, if I am to be a countess it cannot be such a bad bargain."

"Your spirit is all I expected it would be but I shall never forgive myself for putting you in this situation."

"Don't let us talk about it, Papa," she urged him, her voice choked with emotion once again.

There came a faint knock at the door. The valet entered accompanied by a man in a frizzed wig.

"The physician is here, Papa," she told him.

"Why cannot a man be allowed to die in peace?"

"You are not going to die," she answered fiercely.

The physician put down his bag on the bedside and began to open it. Sir John turned his head to look at him with difficulty.

"Did you hear that, Chetwynd? M'daughter hasn't written me off yet, so why have you?"

"You are quite mistaken, sir," answered the physician in a sonorious voice. "I have never intimated by word or deed that you are like to expire, sir."

Sir John chuckled weakly. "You may be a good physician, Chetwynd, but you have no skill in pretending."

"You had best leave us now, madam," suggested the valet.

"What ... is he going to do?"

"Sir John will be better for a cupping," the physician told her.

Jacey looked rather doubtful at the wisdom of that. "He seems so weak."

"Indeed. That is why I deem it necessary to open a vein. You must allow me to know what is best for Sir John."

"I do beg your pardon. This is all such a shock to me."

"Go, Jacey," Sir John urged her. "This is no place for you now. Come back later though, I beg of you."

She pushed back the chair and got to her feet. Leaning forward she kissed his brow. "As soon as Dr Chetwynd has gone I shall return, and I shall also be near at hand in the meantime in the event you should call for me."

"That is a great comfort to me in this time of trial, my lovely."

The valet escorted her to the door. When she reached it she paused to glance back at Sir John who seemed so fragile and unlike the father she had always known.

Outside the bedchamber she leaned wearily against the wall, fighting her tears. Her heart felt as though it was breaking, but whether that was because Sir John was so ill or due to her arranged marriage to the Earl of Sheringham, whom she already hated most heartily, she could not be sure.

Three

Her first night in London was not the joyous one that Jacey had envisaged during that long journey from Cornwall.

The excellent dinner put out for her was left uneaten and she could scarcely wait to return to her father's bedchamber. However, he slept and all she could do was keep vigil until her own fatigue took hold. Mercifully it appeared that he was no worse.

That night she slept only fitfully, despite her exhaustion, her slumber disturbed by visions of coffins and a grotesque mis-shapen creature who called himself Sheringham.

The morning came not a moment too soon and it was only then that she fell into a deep, dreamless sleep at last, waking when her personal maid came in with a cup of chocolate. Alarmed that it was so late, Jacey sat up against the pillows looking anxiously at the maidservant.

"Have you news of Sir John, Rose?"

"Simpson says he's had a comfortable night, ma'am," the girl replied as she busied herself preparing her mistress's toilette.

Jacey then allowed herself a sigh of relief and the luxury of drinking the chocolate. "That is something for which to be grateful."

"Quite a sudden affliction, ma'am, by all accounts," the girl commented as she began to take out a gown from the press. "Came down badly only two nights gone."

"'Tis very strange to me, Rose, for he was ever healthy."

"London air is never that, ma'am, I fear. Fevers abound. Miss Trevallion won't leave her room today, according to Betsey."

"I harbour no fears on her behalf, and I believe it as well that she is indisposed, for her ministrations would be a sore trial to Papa in his present state of health."

She threw back the bedclothes. "I am persuaded it is very late. I must make haste to dress so I can sit with Papa."

"He has already had a visitor this morning."

Jacey was standing in her shift and she turned as the maid slipped the shabby muslin gown over her head.

"That cannot be so, Rose. He is far too ill to receive anyone."

"I can assure you of the truth of it," the girl insisted in outraged tones. "'Twas Simpson himself who told me."

"Who can it have been?" Jacey asked, looking at the maidservant curiously.

"A Lady Moncourt, I believe. I caught sight of her leaving. A very fine lady."

"What can Simpson be thinking of, Rose? Papa is not fit for visitors. He's so desperately ill."

"'Tis odd, ma'am, I own."

Jacey sat down at the dressing table and allowed the maid to dress her hair. "Nothing too elaborate today, Rose, for I am in a fidge to be with Papa again. Oh, it

would break my heart if he were to die now when I am
only just come to London."

"No one has spoken of him dying, ma'am, I'm
sure."

"He thinks he will, and he is so ill, Rose. I know he
is in danger of his life and the worst of it is there is
nought I can do."

As the thought of her coming marriage entered her
mind it was constantly thrust away, for nothing was of
greater import than her father's illness. Even if Lord
Sheringham turned out to be the monster of her
dreams she could not be perturbed by it as long as this
anxiety for Sir John remained.

Almost the moment Rose had finished putting her
hair into a simple coil Jacey was on her feet once more.

"I have dallied long enough. Papa has had notice to
quit, I fear, and I must spend as much time as
possible with him. There might not be much of it left
to us."

She hurried down the corridor and hesitated outside
her father's room. After a moment and seeing the
house-steward in the hall below she hurried down.

"Is Simpson with Sir John, Cranford?"

"Yes, ma'am. He has been upstairs for some time."

All at once Jacey both dreaded and longed to see
her father, fearing after all he would be worse. As she
struggled to compose herself, the door to Sir John's
room opened. Her heart leaped painfully as she looked
up and then her eyes widened scarcely able to believe
what she saw.

There on the landing stood none other than Sir
John Trevallion himself. Far from being about to
expire he was fully dressed in a dark blue superfine
coat, smooth skin tight breeches and a neckcloth

perfectly folded. His hair, which she had last seen matted around his perspiring brow was now a mass of golden curls carefully arranged *à la Brutus*.

"Papa!" she cried in a tone which was plainly disbelieving, as if her eyes were deceiving her.

He looked down to where she was standing and his lips curved into a roguish smile. "Good morning, my lovely."

He walked down the stairs, the tassels on his hessian boots swinging with every step, whilst his daughter continued to look on in astonishment.

"Glad to see you recovered, Sir John," commented the house-steward.

"Thank you, Cranford." Then he turned to his speechless daughter. "How pretty you look this morning."

As she searched his face for signs of his illness he lifted her up and swung her around as he had done so often during her childhood.

"Papa," she gasped as he put her down again, "How can you be in such fine spirits? You were so ill yesterday."

"Are you not pleased to see me here today?" he asked, his eyes twinkling with amusement.

"Indeed, I am, but I don't understand. After being so ill …"

His eyes continued to sparkle as he checked the immaculate folds of his neckcloth in the mirror behind Jacey's head. "A good physick, and the loving concern of a dutiful daughter. 'Tis all the medicine I need. I will take more than an ague to give me notice to quit."

As the house-steward handed him his walking stick, Jacey stepped back, her relief giving way to outrage.

"You old fraud! You humbug! It was all a Banbury Tale, was it not? Did Simpson rub your cheeks with ashes and chalk?"

It was his turn to look bewildered. "I was exceeding ill, you may be sure."

"Foxed more like, and I gave my word because I believed you to be ..."

He cupped her chin in his hand as her voice died away. "Would you rather I go to Peg Trantum after all, eh?"

She pulled away from him in disgust. "I will not quickly forgive you, Papa."

"Next time I vow I shall be gone to Peg Trantum. Will that suit you better, my lovely?"

Stamping her foot on the floor she said, "Why am I cursed with a scoundrel for a father?"

"Now, now," he answered in soothing tones, not at all put out, "I cannot believe you really mean such a sentiment."

She fixed him with a steely eye. "What of Lord Sheringham?"

"Ah, yes, Lord Sheringham." He looked distinctly uneasy then. "I recall we did speak of him at some length." Suddenly he brightened. "The betrothal can be announced with no further delay seeing there is no family mourning to be observed."

Jacey gasped with exasperation. "Aunt Minerva is quite correct about you."

"Oh, yes, I am persuaded she is. Minerva is invariably correct about everything. Where is the dragon lady this morning? Stitching her mourning gown, I don't doubt."

"She is still indisposed by the journey."

He cast her a mocking look. "Naturally. I should have guessed. Ill-health is one of the few things my sister actually enjoys."

As he took his beaver hat from the house-steward she asked a little breathlessly, "As this betrothal is not a spectre in a dying man's mind, when do I meet Lord Sheringham?"

He shrugged slightly. "When your ire has faded a little."

"It will never do that."

He was momentarily startled. "Not towards me, my lovely?"

After moment's hesitation she sighed. "No, Papa. But I have thought there must be another way out of this morass."

"If only there were. This solution only came to me after I had exhausted every other possibility. Even the Jews refuse to accommodate me on this occasion."

"That would be no answer in any event," she told him irritably. "You would merely exchange one dun for another. Perchance, however, I could earn some money."

He looked amused. "The notion is a novel one, but how, pray tell me?"

Her head came up proudly. "I am held to have a pleasant voice. Mayhap I could sing. Pretty voices can become all the crack, I know. I could adopt an Italian name, like the Neopolitan Thrush, or some such creature."

At this suggestion he threw back his head and laughed, which caused her to look hurt.

"No, my lovely; that will not do, I fear. Even if it could be done you would not earn enough in a score of years, and I am persuaded Lord Sheringham will not await his dues so long. In any event if, during my scapegrace existence, I do nothing more I shall see you the Countess of Sheringham."

He was about to step out of the house, but then changed his mind. "If your aunt is up to it let her accompany you to Bond Street. You look a trifle shabby and I would not have you go to the altar a dowd."

"One needs money, Papa, to buy fashionable clothes."

"There is no problem, my lovely. The future Countess of Sheringham will have no trouble obtaining credit in any establishment she cares to patronise. They'll grease your boots quite willingly, you'll find."

Jacey couldn't help but laugh. "Papa, you are incorrigible. I have no intention of doing any such thing."

He gave her a searching look. "Do as you please as long as you don't hate me."

"As if I could."

She went to him and he cradled her close for a moment or two before holding her away, saying, "This will never do. Here, take this." He reached into his pocket and brought out a purse which he placed in her hands.

"What is this?" she asked, gazing at it curiously.

"Exactly what it appears to be. Money. Buy yourself a new gown and a bonnet to match, of course."

Jacey looked astonished then. "But, Papa, I thought your pockets are to let."

"So they are, but there's enough for you to buy yourself a few gee-gaws."

She sighed and shook her head. "I couldn't, Papa."

He refused to take it back and moved away from her before she could press it on him. "You cannot meet your bridegroom in outmoded gowns, my lovely. However, I cannot delay any longer. I have a deal of business which needs my attention."

"Faro or hazard?" she asked, eyeing him wryly.

He held up one hand. "I am a reformed man, Jacey. No more gaming for me, I vow."

She cast him a disbelieving look and as he sauntered towards the door he added, glancing over his shoulder, "Be ready when I return this afternoon and I shall take you riding in the Park."

Shaking her head in exasperation she watched him go, and then her smile faded somewhat. One worry had disappeared but that left her with nothing else to consider but the prospect of being married to the unseen Earl of Sheringham.

Jacey wondered frantically how that could be averted without inviting disastrous results for her father. A sudden vision of him languishing in the Fleet Prison filled her heart with hatred anew, and she wondered how she could ever bear to be married to such a heartless man.

Four

"Betsey tells me your father has been quite ill." Minerva Trevallion, cosily ensconced in the four-poster bed looked up from her sewing as Jacey came across the room and eased herself into a chair at the bedside.

"He is fully recovered now."

"I am relieved, for I cannot recall him ever being ill before. He enjoys the rudest health, although why I cannot conceive, for his rackety way of living is not conducive to it."

"It was a mere bagatelle, Aunt, and nothing with which you should trouble your head."

"Good. It was always I who was the delicate one in the family. My constitution is not at all strong, as you well know."

"You are looking much better today, though."

"I own that I am. I shall rise tomorrow and resume my guardianship once more. Whatever the state of my health, I should always hope to be steadfast in my duty."

"You may not be burdened for much longer, Aunt."

The spinster looked up and her eyes narrowed. "Do you think finding a husband is such an easy task?"

"Easier than I had imagined," she replied wryly.

"Papa has arranged a match for me."

Miss Trevallion's hand flew to her lips. "Glory be! I cannot credit this. My brother is executing his duty at last."

"Not quite, Aunt Minerva. It seems my portion is to settle Papa's gaming debts and as you are aware that cannot be until I become leg-shackled."

The woman sank back into the pillows growing pale. "Good grief! It is worse than anything I had supposed. The poltroon. My vinaigrette, Jacey. I declare I am about to expire."

Unperturbed, Jacey reached out to where the vinaigrette was always to hand and gave it to her aunt.

After a few moments Miss Trevallion was sufficiently recovered to say, "My poor, poor child. What are you to do?"

"Marry him, naturally. What else am I to do?"

"That is uncharacteristically complaisant of you."

"I have promised Papa that I will marry this Lord Sheringham. I cannot now break my word, nor would I wish to. Papa would be in the direst trouble. Do you know the Earl of Sheringham, Aunt?"

"I do not. The less I know of your Papa's rackety friends the better I am satisfied. How could he do such a thing?"

"For Papa it is easy. He does not mean to do anything wrong; he cannot help himself."

Miss Trevallion eyed Jacey curiously now. "You are remarkably calm about it."

"Railing would only distress us all and not alter the situation, but I do have hopes it will come to nought. I am not wed yet. Despite his declaration that he will no longer gamble, Papa may win a fortune." She brightened. "Lord Sheringham might die; he might even dislike me on sight." She sighed then. "That will not do; it would only put Papa in an impossible situation."

"A spell in the Fleet might do him good."

"How would he get out?"

"He wouldn't," Miss Trevallion answered with a great deal of satisfaction.

"You would not enjoy seeing him in such a situation."

Miss Trevallion shook her head in amazement. "Jacey, you should be hating him for putting this blight on your future, instead of always making excuses for him."

"I cannot, somehow, hold him to blame, Aunt, and I do adore him."

"Females," she scoffed. "We are ever foolish to be prey to the charm of men."

Jacey smiled. "Yes, I know you adore him, too."

Indignantly she pulled her shawl about her and Jacey went on in a soft voice, "I really do feel, Aunt Minerva, that somewhere, somehow, there is a way out of this morass."

"Then you had best discover it quickly, for Lord Sheringham will not wait idly by for his debt to settled."

"I can only hope he will wait but a little while. In any event I must endeavour to enjoy this Season whilst I can. Papa is taking me riding in the Park this afternoon."

"Hah! Everyone will think you one of his lightskirts, I don't doubt."

Not at all put out, Jacey got to her feet. "Not in my shabby gown, Aunt Minerva, so have no fear."

When she reached the door Miss Trevallion called

out, "You may tell your father that when I leave this bed he is going to receive the benefit of my frank opinion of his behaviour."

Jacey chuckled. "He fears that, Aunt Minerva, more than a spell in the Fleet."

* * *

Sir John Trevallion's phaeton and pair bowled along Oxford Street at a spanking pace. Seated beside him Jacey viewed her surroundings with scarce-concealed glee.

"Glad you came?" he asked, glancing at her sideways as the phaeton swerved to avoid an oncoming carriage.

"I've been longing to come for two years and more. I thought of little else in Cornwall."

"Can't think why I didn't send for you before."

"I dare say you were always too busy," she answered bluntly, "and didn't wish to trouble your head with a green girl like me."

"There's a mite of truth in that, although I have always been proud of you, but after your mother died I lost interest in everything. Tried to forget by filling my time with trivial diversions. I should have spent more time with you. You've grown up without my realising it."

"You should have remarried."

"Never found anyone like your mother."

"You wouldn't need to. There must be many worthy females with whom you could find a congenial existence."

He glanced at her. "I would have thought you wouldn't much fancy the idea of a step-mother."

"It is what is right for you which concerns me. In any event, I shall soon be wed with an establishment of my own, whatever it may be." When he made no further comment she ventured, "Does he know I am in London?"

Sir John shrugged. "He must be aware that your arrival is imminent."

He looked acutely uncomfortable but nevertheless Jacey persisted, "What is Lord Sheringham like, Papa?"

"What a crack-brained question," he answered, laughing gruffly. "As if I am able to import an opinion. You will see for yourself in due course."

His evasiveness did nothing to ease Jacey's doubts, but her mind was somewhat diverted by the sight of so many of the *beau monde* as the phaeton bowled into Hyde Park at the height of the fashionable hour.

The paths were crowded with a vast miscellany of carriages, all of them beautifully appointed. No more overshadowed were the magnificent horses drawing them. Jacey's eyes opened wide at the sight of so much splendour, the people all dressed in the finest stuff whether they rode or walked.

"Now I really do feel a dowd," she cried.

He glanced at her as the phaeton was obliged to slow to a walking pace because of the crowded paths. "I did tell you to buy yourself something new to wear."

"Oh, I couldn't, Papa. Not when you're so short of funds."

"Allow me to worry about the blunt, Jacey. You should not trouble your pretty head on such matters."

"I cannot help myself."

"Just look at my coat. Feel the superfine." She did

so. "Weston made that for me – the best tailor in Town. Not only that, but I engage Brummel's bootmaker. You can't say your Papa doesn't buy rum rigging."

"I cannot conceive how you contrive."

"It is quite simple, I assure you, my dear. Pay a little, take a lot."

She shook her head although she could not help but laugh. "You are incorrigible, Papa, you really are."

"And you are, my lovely, the finest daughter a man could have. I am very proud of you."

Her cheeks grew rather pink. All around them people were calling out to him and all the while he acknowledged their greetings with a gay flourish of his whip, or in the case of a lady by raising his curly-brimmed beaver. Jacey smiled rather absently at them and although she was receiving curious glances all around surprisingly Sir John didn't attempt to stop and engage any of them in conversation.

A moment later he said in an unusually serious tone, "Jacey, I really do feel very bad about this business with Sheringham."

She subjected him to a steady look. "Do you really, Papa?"

"You must know it is so, Jacey."

She smiled then. "Good. At least I can be content in that."

"Hell and damnation, Jacey! If the notion of becoming leg-shackled to Sheringham is so abhorrent to you, you shall be allowed to cry off."

For a moment she didn't reply and then she said, "And have you languish in the Fleet? I'd as lief become leg-shackled to the Devil."

He stared at her in astonishment and then suddenly

she caught sight of a curricle coming towards them. Jacey sat up straight so she could view it the better. It was not the man tooling the ribbons who caught her eye; the female passenger was one of the most beautiful she had ever seen.

As the curricle approached it slowed even more and when the two men raised their hats, the woman smiled, inclining her head slightly to Sir John. In response he urged his team on the faster and their carriages passed with scarce a pause. Jacey turned her head when the curricle had passed, following its progress, and she was not alone in her interest. The curricle's passage was inviting a deal of interest all around it.

At last Jacey returned her attention to her father, but she scarcely noted that his cheeks had grown red. "Who was that?"

"To whom do you refer?" he asked and to her astonishment appeared acutely discomforted.

"The lady in the curricle which has just passed us by."

"The lady? Oh, yes, the lady."

"I declare I have never seen anyone so beautiful. And her bonnet; so many feathers."

"You shall have one even better," he vowed.

"I doubt if it would suit me. She must be a duchess."

Sir John smiled and seemed to have relaxed somewhat. "She is fetching, is she not?"

"Then you are acquainted with her?"

He chuckled. "Not as well as I would wish. Her name is Mollie Dinsdale, but she is no duchess."

He chuckled again and after gazing at him curiously Jacey's cheeks began to redden and she averted her eyes.

"If they are all as beautiful as that lady it is no wonder cyprians are pursued by gentlemen of means."

"One has to be of considerable means to pursue Mollie Dinsdale."

"I am persuaded lack of funds never inhibited *you*, Papa."

"No, indeed. I should hope not. Your Mama never cared a jot for money either, even after her portion and her jewellery were gone."

"Neither do I. I only wish my own portion was not entailed to my husband. Sheringham could have it and welcome."

He glanced at her and gave her a regretful smile. "I wish that were so, too, my lovely."

"But at least this way you will not be cast into the Fleet. I couldn't bear that."

"Nor could I," he answered with a sigh, directing the phaeton towards the nearest gate. "Damned smelly place, by all accounts."

Her eyes became troubled. "Surely Lord Sheringham wouldn't be so heartless ..."

"Afraid he would, my lovely. He's not like me, you know. That's why he is always in funds and I am not. I haven't the heart to go dunning people."

"He sounds like an abomination."

Sir John laughed uneasily. "Now now, my lovely, don't get the wrong impression of the fellow; he's not the coxcomb you suppose."

Jacey glanced at him as the phaeton made its way down Oxford Street, back towards Bedford Square, not at all reassured.

Five

"Do look at all these invitations, Aunt Minerva!"
Jacey's eyes were aglow as she put them on the
breakfast table and then sat down to peruse them the
better.

"There will be a great deal of curiosity about you,
my dear," her aunt replied, returning to her hearty
breakfast.

"It is what I had always dreamed of, Aunt.
Invitations to the homes of the *ton*."

"Dreams often turn into nightmares," her aunt
predicted darkly. "There will be time for you to
examine those cards later. Eat your breakfast before it
grows cold. A good breakfast is essential to rude
health. You know that I firmly believe in that."

Despite her aunt's strictures Jacey could not help
but continue to look at the invitations which had been
left in the hall. Her smile faded slightly for none of the
cards had come from Lord Sheringham. It was a relief
to her but a puzzlement too. She imagined he would
be curious about his future wife, even anxious.

"There is a ball at Lord and Lady Dunscombe of
Grosvenor Square," she gasped as she reached the
invitation. "I dare say that will be a veritable
hurricane."

Miss Trevallion sniffed derisively. "Unhealthy gatherings. Stuffy crowded places. No wonder there is so much pestilence in London."

Jacey gave her a look of dismay. "Oh, do not say we cannot go, Aunt Minerva."

Miss Trevallion indicated to the attendant footman to refill her cup. "I dare say your Papa will insist upon our going, although why I cannot imagine; you are, after all, betrothed."

Jacey buttered a slice of toast before thickly coating it with honey. "I beg of you not to remind me of *that*. At least I am not yet leg-shackled."

"You can scarce forget it. Trevallion indicated to me last night that the wedding will take place in a month's time, and for once he was sober."

Her niece's face took on a stricken look. Her eggs and toast remained uneaten on the plate.

"Oh dear! So soon."

"If the event is to take place at all, why delay unduly? And in view of the circumstances I dare say there will be some haste involved."

"I had thought of it as some evil day far away, Aunt."

"For that I cannot blame you, my dear, but, tell me, have you learned anything more about Lord Sheringham?"

"Papa avoids any mention of him, so I am bound to fear the worst. A monster. He must be."

"Mis-shapen, you mean?" her aunt asked in a conversational tone. "Knowing your father's cronies I shouldn't doubt it."

Jacey looked suddenly thoughtful. "Papa's cronies are invariably Corinthians, Aunt, but that does not mean to say he always games with *them*. I have no doubt that Sheringham is at least five and fifty, stout and ill-tempered with the gout. How can it be otherwise for a man to agree to wed a green girl he has never seen?"

Miss Trevallion peered at her over the Dunscombe's invitation which she had been perusing. "You are obviously unoptimistic about your future."

She managed a smile. "That is not so, Aunt. After all, if Lord Sheringham is as I believe him to be he will soon be given notice to quit, leaving me a widow, will he not?"

Miss Trevallion gave a gruff laugh at her niece's reasoning. "I doubt if he will be so obliging."

"I live in hope – if the wedding cannot after all be averted – that he will be good enough to allow me to go my own way. It is only a business arrangement and no feelings are involved. I believe it is quite a common arrangement in some of the best families; one only has to look at the Royal Family – and the Prince of Wales himself."

Her aunt shuddered. "Oh, please, I beg of you, do not hold that coxcomb up as an example. Poor Princess Caroline; how badly he uses her."

"Well, I am more concerned for my own marriage. I will find a way of making it congenial, if – as I have said – it does have to be entered into."

"You father is a most fortunate fellow to have such an obliging daughter, and I have told him so."

Jacey began to eat at last. "If I am not mistaken, Aunt, you told him last night, for I have rarely seen him so Friday-faced."

Miss Trevallion sat back in her chair. "You may be certain that I gave him a set-down, but," she added with a sigh, "that cannot help you now. Pray allow me to see those other invitations."

Obligingly her niece passed them across the table. For a few moments Miss Trevallion shuffled through them in silence before declaring, "This card party at Lady Grossington's looks to be interesting." Jacey pulled a wry face. "And I suppose we shall be obliged to attend Lord and Lady Beechwood's rout. Oh dear, have you seen this one?"

Jacey looked up from her breakfast. "Which one, Aunt? I have scarce glanced at them yet. I am being obedient and eating my breakfast as you bade me."

"You must stop at once and consider this." She peered short-sightedly at the card and began to read. "The Marchioness of Moncourt requests the pleasure of the Misses Trevallion at two of the clock at Moncourt House, Park Lane on the twenty-ninth."

As Jacey listened her aunt looked up. "Why, that is today!"

The girl frowned and put down her fork. "The Marchioness of Moncourt? Do we know of her?"

"I certainly do not."

"I feel that I know the name and yet how could I?" Her eyes suddenly opened wide. "Indeed I do, Aunt! It was Lady Moncourt who visited Papa in his sick room the first morning after our arrival in London!"

Miss Trevallion's thin lips twisted into a sneer. "His sick bed, indeed! The effects of too much imbibing, more like."

Jacey chuckled, having entirely forgiven Sir John the fright he had given her. "He was so afraid you would visit him."

"Naturally. He knows I am up to snuff and would not be deceived by his play-acting."

"Even if you had it would have made no odds, Aunt."

"You might not have felt obliged to give your word to marry Lord Sheringham."

"I would have done so in any event."

Miss Trevallion shook her head sadly. "His tongue is well hung. He could charm the birds from the trees if he wished." She glanced again at Lady Moncourt's invitation. "I had best write a note crying off this engagement, Jacey."

Her niece looked outraged. "Why, Aunt?"

"Because we are both too shabby to visit someone so obviously as grand as Lady Moncourt."

"Tush! Our clothing may not be of the most fashionable, but it is clean. If we are not accepted as we are, then I cannot be sorry."

Miss Trevallion cast her an ironic look as she gathered together the cards and got up from the table.

"I think you mean if Lord Sheringham will not accept you, my dear." Jacey looked away. "I fear to tell you that he would accept you clad in a coachman's frieze coat, providing your portion is large enough."

As she swept out of the room Jacey's expression became a vexed one and angrily she pushed her breakfast plate away from her.

* * *

Sir John's shabby carriage drew up outside the palatial frontage of Moncourt House, which overlooked Hyde Park, at precisely two o'clock that afternoon.

It was very difficult for Jacey not to be impressed

and she was very nearly overwhelmed by the magnificence of the hall which dwarfed both her aunt and herself. She looked up at the domed ceiling far above them, at the marble pillars and niches where statues of mythological characters were ensconced.

A footman in scarlet and gold livery led the way up one half of the double curving staircase and Jacey felt all at once nervous as she and her aunt waited outside a pair of double doors to be admitted to Lady Moncourt's private sitting room.

"I am persuaded I shall become tongue-tied out of sheer fright," Jacey confided in a whisper.

Her aunt cast her a wry glance. "The day I see you as mute as a fish will be an odd one indeed."

Stepping inside at last they found themselves in a large room, furnished with the most elegant mahogany furniture. As the double doors closed behind them a voice from the far end of the room called out for them to come forward.

Aunt Minerva sketched a curtsey and almost as an afterthought Jacey followed suit. She believed that her aunt was as overwhelmed as she.

The walk down the room seemed to be a mile long. Now she was actually here Jacey felt even more apprehensive. She had heard of those vastly wealthy and influential ladies of the *ton*, but now to be faced with one at close quarters was a terrifying prospect.

Lady Moncourt was reclining on a day bed, clad in a pink gown of figured chiffon. She wore a turban on her head and its six feathers exactly matched the colour of her gown. At her heel sat a turbanned page wearing the scarlet and gold livery of the house, but he was as black as coal.

As they approached, Lady Moncourt put down her

fan and Jacey was at last able to see her properly. She was younger than Jacey had expected and more handsome in appearance than beautiful, but her figure was well-rounded. Jacey was all at once admiring, but she was still overawed.

"Do be seated, ladies," their hostess invited, and her voice was soft and melodious.

Jacey and her aunt obeyed, sitting together on a sofa which faced both Lady Moncourt and the fire that roared up the chimney. Jacey's hands, hidden within her muff, were clasped together apprehensively.

"Sir John has told me a great deal about you both. I am so pleased to see you at last."

"It is gracious of you to extend an invitation, my lady."

It was Miss Trevallion who had answered. Jacey just gazed at Lady Moncourt in awe until the marchioness smiled at her and seemed then to be not the least bit alarming.

"I am only pleased that you were able to accept my invitation at such short notice. I know that you will be inundated by invitations and calls from now on."

"Yes, indeed, my lady. We have already begun to receive them."

"You do not surprise me at all. At times I believe all the hurry-scurry to meet newcomers to Town is rather unseemly. A glass of ratafia, ladies?"

Before either of them could answer she had prodded the page with the toe of her slipper and he sprang to his feet, handing around the glasses.

"You visited my father the other day," Jacey ventured, her curiosity overcoming her timidity.

"I heard that he was ill and was quite alarmed, for

it is unlike him, I own."

That observation caused Jacey to exchange a glance with her aunt before replying, "That is certainly true, my lady."

The marchioness sipped at her ratafia. "You can imagine that I was most gratified to find him recovered." She looked then at Miss Trevallion. "It is, I understand, a considerable interval since your last visit to Town, Miss Trevallion."

"All of twenty years, my lady."

"No doubt you will have found life a little different to how it was then."

"By no means. Apart from the mode of dressing, which is a good deal more simple, little has changed, my lady."

The marchioness transferred her attention to Jacey again and startled her by saying, "You are very lovely, my dear. Trevallion has been remiss in not bringing you to Town much sooner."

Jacey flushed at such praise and as she averted her eyes she replied, "I think it remiss of him too, my lady."

"However, now that he has seen fit to bring you to Town we must ensure that your time is spent profitably. In other words," she added, a twinkle in her eye, "we must make certain you have every opportunity to meet eligible young men. After all, that is why you are here, I take it. Matrimony must surely be any young lady's goal."

Once again Jacey exchanged an alarmed look with her aunt who replied, looking uncharacteristically discomforted, "My niece is already betrothed, my lady."

At this disclosure Lady Moncourt sat up straight,

swinging her legs over the side of the day bed. "Is she indeed? Trevallion never said so. He is exceeding neglectful, I fear. A man from Cornwall, perchance?"

"No, he is not, my lady."

It was Jacey who spoke, but when the marchioness raised her eyebrows interrogatively, Miss Trevallion supplied, "My niece is betrothed to the Earl of Sheringham."

Lady Moncourt's eyes opened wide. Jacey guessed that there would be few occasions when she was nonplussed.

"Sheringham! Oh, surely not. You are gammoning me, are you not?"

As she laughed disparagingly Jacey shifted uncomfortably in her seat. "I assure you, my lady, we do not jest."

"Sheringham. I cannot credit such a thing. Why did I not know of it?"

"It is not yet announced, my lady," Miss Trevallion hastened to assure her.

The marchioness's eyes narrowed. "There is more to this than you will own. Trevallion has been in an odd humour of late, not to mention being as close as an oak, and I'll warrant it is in some way connected to this betrothal."

Jacey gave her a curious look. "You appear to know Papa very well, Lady Moncourt."

The marchioness smiled in a very revealing way. The sight of that smile jolted Jacey somewhat.

"Oh, indeed; Trevallion and I have been acquainted for a long time. Now, tell me about your betrothal to Sheringham. I am in a fidge to know how it came about. When did you meet? In Cornwall? I am persuaded Trevallion did not entertain there, and yet it cannot have been in Town or everyone would know of it by now."

Miss Trevallion looked discomforted and Jacey, drawing in a sigh replied, "I do not see why Lady Moncourt should not be told, Aunt Minerva."

"Your Papa ..."

"Tush." She looked at Lady Moncourt whose eyes remained wide. "It is an arranged marriage."

The marchioness stiffened. "Arranged! Are marriages arranged nowadays?" When neither of them answered she went on, "Sheringham has no need to wed a fortune and yet there is something quite odd about the situation. You must forgive me for saying so," she added.

"Naturally, Lady Moncourt," Jacey replied, feeling acutely discomforted.

"Then I shall not ask if you are madly in love with him, Miss Trevallion. I would not be so insensitive but you are evidently sufficiently impressed by him to agree to this marriage." When neither ladies replied, Lady Moncourt asked in a hesitant way, "You have met Lord Sheringham?"

"Not as yet," Jacey admitted heavily.

Lady Moncourt got to her feet and began to walk around. Suddenly she began to chuckle. "This is famous. I cannot conceive what he is about, but I am persuaded Trevallion's attic is to let."

"That is very like," Minerva Trevallion agreed.

The marchioness then turned once again to Jacey. "You must think me heartless, my dear, to laugh."

"Not at all, my lady. If I were not embroiled so closely in this, I should also find it amusing."

Obviously regretful the marchioness came to sit at Jacey's side, taking her hand. "My dear, I only laugh because your father, who is very dear to me, is for ever hatching crack-brained schemes. This seems the most buffle headed of all although I had never considered Sheringham to be the kind of man to go along with one." After pausing a moment she asked, "Is it to do with his being in dun territory?"

Jacey nodded and Miss Trevallion drew in a sharp breath. "Jacey, really!"

"Oh, I do understand your outrage, Miss Trevallion," the marchioness assured her, "but you need have no fear. What you tell me here today will go no further than the three of us."

"You relieve me, my lady," Miss Trevallion answered stiffly, obviously still outraged.

"*On-dits* only bear recounting when they do not affect a person of whom one is fond."

Jacey looked at her in amazement as she went on quickly, "Am I to assume you are not much in favour of this match, my dear?"

Jacey stiffened. "You are quite mistaken, my lady."

Lady Moncourt drew back and then got up, going slowly back to her day bed. When she turned around again she asked brightly, "Do tell me about all your social engagements, ladies. I do trust you are being received cordially into the homes of the *ton*."

Relieved at the change in conversation Jacey and Miss Trevallion eagerly began to tell her of all the invitations they had so far received and after a pleasant half hour of bland conversation the Misses Trevallion took leave of their hostess.

As they settled into the carriage Aunt Minerva said crossly, "Really, Jacey, you should not have told Lady Moncourt the circumstances of your betrothal."

"I did not."

"You told her a great deal."

"Why should I not? It is not something of which I need to be ashamed."

"It most certainly is, and now Lady Moncourt will ensure that everyone will know of it."

Jacey sank into the squabs as the carriage jerked into motion, a strange smile playing at the corners of her lips.

"I cannot see how that will be, Aunt. After all, Lady Moncourt has given us her word to remain silent on the matter."

"Tush. Her social standing rests on her being able to reveal the latest tattle to her acquaintances. That is why she wished to be first to invite us into her home."

"No doubt, but I believe she will keep her word on this occasion."

Miss Trevallion smiled faintly. "You are exceeding trusting, my dear. A few weeks in this town will soon remedy that, I fancy."

Jacey remained undismayed, gazing out of the carriage window. "Aunt Minerva, after what Papa and this Lord Sheringham have arranged between them I harbour no illusions about what can go on in this Town. However, in this instance I can be adamant, for if I am not mistaken Lady Moncourt is actually in love with Papa."

Miss Trevallion started. "What a ridiculous assumption! How can you think such a thing of her? She seems full of good sense."

Jacey chuckled. "Sensible females are usually the ones who throw their caps over the windmill more readily."

Her aunt looked both surprised and irritated. "You cannot possibly know."

"It is not impossible. Papa is very handsome."

"Mayhap he is, but even so not everyone is enamoured of that poltroon."

"But Lady Moncourt is," Jacey insisted, smiling contentedly, her mind working at a furious rate.

"And there, I believe, is the road to my salvation," she added, almost under her breath, causing her aunt to stare at her in astonishment.

Six

"What a beautiful gown, ma'am."

The garment in question was lying across Jacey's bed and she looked at it then at her maid, and back to the gown again. The gown of white *crêpe de chine*, embroidered with seed pearls and crystal, was indeed exquisite. Jacey stared at it for a few moments before snatching up the note by its side.

"Wear it for me, my lovely."

Dropping the note back on to the bed Jacey drew a sigh. "This is madness. He cannot afford the expense of a gown of this magnificence."

"You needs must wear it for Lord and Lady Dunscombe's ball, ma'am. Everyone there will be in their finest. Lord Sheringham may well be there, too."

That thought had been haunting Jacey since the arrival of the invitation, but she answered in a calm enough tone, "I am persuaded that he might be and therefore had made up my mind to go as shabby as I could contrive."

Rose laughed. "You couldn't do that, ma'am, not even if you tried."

Jacey sighed. "My aunt declares it makes no odds how I appear, so I may as well please Papa."

His pleasure in her appearance was evident when she walked down the stairs to find him waiting in the hall. She was wearing the gown, her golden curls dressed around a garland of flowers.

"A vision of loveliness. You will rival the greatest beauty in the land tonight."

"Faddle. I am not so receptive to your flummery as your lightskirts, Papa."

His eyes opened wide. "Jacey, what have I done to deserve such a set-down?"

Her face relaxed into a smile. "Nothing, Papa," she answered, giving him a quick kiss on the cheek.

He rubbed his hands together gleefully. "You will have every man agog tonight," he declared as she pulled on her gloves.

"And what use is that, may I ask? You might just as well have saved the blunt, for I am persuaded Sheringham will not mind how I look."

"To the Devil with Sheringham; *I* wish to see you in high feather."

As his sister came down the stairs to join them, Sir John became rather less ebullient.

"You have used your daughter most abominably," she accused immediately.

A fleeting look of irritation crossed his face. "Now, now, Minerva, do not go on again, or I declare I shall cry off this evening."

"That is typical of you, Trevallion, to run away."

"I go only for the sake of you and your niece, madam, so I pray you display a little more gratitude than I observe now. I'd as lief be at my club."

"Gaming away whose portion this time?"

His face grew red under his sister's disapprobation

and it was then that Jacey put up her hand. "Oh, please, Aunt Minerva, Papa, don't quarrel, I beg of you. What is done is done. Let us enjoy my first ball in Town."

Sir John lookd mollified and put his arm around his daughter's waist. "She is splendid, is she not? A creature of rare spirit. How fortunate Sheringham will be."

"She is more than *you* deserve," was his sister's parting shot.

When the carriage was on its way to Grosvenor Square, Jacey cast him a sideways glance. He looked quite handsome in his dark blue evening coat and satin breeches. She didn't wonder that Lady Moncourt was enamoured of him. The passage of years seemed hardly to have touched him, and she was more than ever determined to see him settled into matrimony before the ravages of dissipation made themselves apparent.

"We called upon Lady Moncourt yesterday, Papa," she ventured and he started.

"Maria Moncourt? Why ...?"

"She condescended to extend an invitation."

"We found her amiable in the extreme," Miss Trevallion broke in, nodding her head sagely.

"Oh, she is," he agreed. "She is. Most agreeable; none more so."

"We were surprised to find her so well-acquainted with you, Papa," Jacey mused.

He squirmed slightly in his seat. "Oh, indeed."

Her aunt cast her a knowing look but Jacey persisted, "Are you also acquainted with Lord Moncourt?"

"Good grief no. The poor fellow has been dead for years."

"It is evident that he left her with a well-lined purse."

"Lady Moncourt is as rich as can be, you may be sure," he answered, sighing deeply.

At this confirmation Jacey also drew a sigh, one of satisfaction.

After a moment's silence she went on, "What a pity your regard for her isn't great enough to consider a closer relationship than you have at present."

Miss Trevallion drew in a sharp breath and shot her a warning look. Her brother started nervously.

"Good grief, Jacey, what are you suggesting?"

"Widowers have been known to wed widows, especially when they are as fetching as Lady Moncourt."

Sir John became even more perturbed. He seemed to find his neckcloth suddenly rather tight. "Marriage? My dear, you are gammoning me."

"What else did you think I meant?" she asked, her eyes opening wide.

"You have no notion of the matter. My pockets are to let. How could one such as I consider matrimony to one as wealthy as Maria Moncourt?"

"It would seem to be an ideal arrangement. Marriage to her would result in your becoming wealthy too."

He looked unusually vexed. "Dammit, Jacey, a man has his pride."

She drew in a sigh once more. She was not at all dismayed. Pride could be overcome, she was certain.

The road had become congested with carriages, all en route for Dunscombe House. Jacey sat back to await impatiently their turn to climb down.

"Papa, is Lord Sheringham like to be at the ball tonight?"

He flinched at the mention of the earl's name and seemed to sink further down into the squabs. "How should I know? The fellow's damnably elusive these days. I have had no success in contacting him since your arrival."

"He has no more notion of what I am like than I have of him. 'Tis most remarkable that he agreed to this match."

Off-handedly Sir John replied, "He has seen the miniature of you that I always keep by me, although," he added, "he was a trifle foxed at the time."

Jacey couldn't help but laugh. "But that is several years old. I am utterly changed."

"Well, he could see you had no visible defects."

"That is no guarantee. Painters invariably flatter their sitters for it is they who pay and would not do so if portrayed as ugly."

"That is of no consequence. No painter could do you true justice and in any event you have grown far more beautiful and he cannot be anything other than totally enchanted."

Jacey was angered by the thought. "It is nothing to me if he takes me in dislike."

"But it means everything to me, recall. If he is present tonight, Jacey, you had best make yourself amenable, for if he decides he does not wish to marry you after all, I shall be frying in my own grease in the Fleet Prison."

"You expect far too much of her," his sister broke in. "You presented the poor child with a *fait accompli*; Jacey has had no choice in this matter which I declare is most shabby of you."

"Oh, do hold your tongue, madam," he replied irritably. "You should not attempt to incite m'daughter to defy me."

"As if I could," she scoffed.

Jacey sighed. "Have no fear, Papa, for I shall not cause you any heartache in that direction, and you have ensured I do not look a dowd."

"You look quite splendid, my lovely. I wish that I still had your Mama's diamonds for you to wear."

"Since they crossed the baize years ago," Miss Trevallion again broke in, much to his irritation, "my own pearls will have to do."

He looked downhearted for a moment or two but then he rallied and said, "I am as always proud of my girl, with or without jewels."

He leaned forward and stroked her cheek with one finger. She cast him a fond smile but her eager anticipation of the Dunscombe's ball was overshadowed now by thoughts of Lord Sheringham.

* * *

The salons of Dunscombe House were crowded and Jacey wandered through them wide-eyed. If anything, it was more splendid than Lady Moncourt's mansion. However on this occasion she did not feel the least out of place. Her gown was as fine as any worn there that night and she had been accorded a good deal of attention.

Sir John had introduced her to a bewildering number of his acquaintances until Lady Moncourt arrived to claim him for one of the sets, which pleased Jacey a good deal. Accordingly she had melted away

into the crowds in order that the marchioness should
have her father's undivided attention. By that time
Miss Trevallion was playing whist and, uneasy again,
Jacey was viewing every gentleman present as a
possible Lord Sheringham. Of course, many of the
younger gentlemen were very presentable but
somehow Jacey did not think that one of them could
be the earl.

Not a few guests were eyeing her, too. She didn't
doubt that news of her betrothal was beginning to leak
out despite her father's close-lipped attitude to the
subject. It suited her that few people knew of it, for
when she succeeded in marrying Sir John to Lady
Moncourt, it would be easier to break off the
betrothal.

Jacey was utterly convinced that this was the ideal
answer to her dilemma. Her father's pride was a great
obstacle in that direction, but she guessed Lady
Moncourt was a determined lady, too, and with a little
encouragement, it could be overcome.

A stout gentleman was viewing her through a
quizzing glass. She had noticed his interest in one of
the other rooms and all at once she became uneasy at
his persistent presence nearby. As she dithered
uncertainty he approached her at last. She looked with
disdain at his garish coat with its paste buttons and at
the back of her mind lurked an unspeakable fear.

"Miss Trevallion," he bowed.

"Sir?" she asked uneasily.

He smiled. "May I bespeak the cotillion?"

"Yes ... but to whom shall I credit the set? I don't
recall being introduced."

"No, indeed. In the salon the crush around you was
too great. I was anxious to make your acquaintance,

naturally."

"Naturally ...?"

He gave her a bewildered smile. "Everyone is most anxious to make the acquaintance of Sir John Trevallion's daughter, especially as it is now apparent she is so charming."

She smiled uneasily. "You are too kind, sir."

"That cannot be. Sir John and I are old friends. I dare say he might have mentioned my name to you. We throw the dice together on occasions." Jacey drew in a sharp breath, as he bowed again, "Cedric Crumleigh-Smyth, ma'am, always at your service."

She let out a great sigh of relief as he wandered away. However, there were several hundred other men present and most of them were not of a prepossessing character.

Suddenly another presence at her side caused her to turn around in alarm.

"My country dance, Miss Trevallion."

Her head was almost light with relief at the sight of a young man to whom she had been introduced earlier. He was one gentleman who had found favour in her eyes, for he was quite handsome and his mode of dress left nothing to be desired. He was all elegance and charm. However, she did know him not to be the Earl of Sheringham.

"Mr. Pringle," she responded. "I should be delighted."

His company and the dance served to divert her mind for a while, for he was an attentive and amusing partner. After the country dance had ended she was reluctant to part with him but they were both engaged elsewhere.

However as he took his leave of her at the edge of the dance floor he looked deep into her eyes, saying, "Miss Trevallion, we shall meet again later."

The promise made her shiver with delight, and later when she was engaged for more of the dances she began to think less of Lord Sheringham, for she had made up her mind he would not after all be present. Through the milling crowds she was glad enough to see her father often in the company of Lady Moncourt. The only problem with this state of affairs being her inability to know whether that was usual or not, and in any event conversing in a crowded ballroom was not conducive to the kind of intimacy she was anxious to promote.

Jacey was soon breathless and flushed after standing up for a series of dances. Not for her, it seemed, the ignominy of being obliged to sit out most of the the sets.

A rather handsome gentleman, exquisitely dressed, was approaching. Fleetingly Jacey thought she wouldn't mind at all if this turned out to be Lord Sheringham. Many other eyes watched him admiringly as he made his way through the room, although he made no attempt to acknowledge any of those attempting to accost him.

He bowed briefly to Jacey. "Miss Trevallion, my compliments. Your conduct is most becoming."

Breathlessly she answered, "I thank you, sir, but have I had the honour of making your acquaintance?"

He smiled faintly, waving a languid hand in the air. The movement had about it the air of a carefully studied gesture.

"Your ignorance of my identity does you credit, Miss,

Trevallion. It pleases me greatly. I am slightly acquainted with Sir John Trevallion. We did on one occasion play at the tables together.''

Her heart jerked unevenly as he bowed stiffly again. "George Brummel at your service, madam.''

Before she had realised it he had gone, leaving her stunned at the side of the dance floor. Beau Brummel, she repeated to herself. That was the famed Brummel himself. She put her hand up to her scarlet cheeks as a young woman of about her own age came hurrying up to her, fluttering a fan.

Jacey had noticed her before, auburn-haired and sadly affllicted with a multitude of freckles.

"Miss Trevallion, you are indeed honoured,'' she said haughtily and in a manner which indicated she was envious, too. "Brummel does not condescend to converse with many, you may be certain.''

"Yes, I know,'' she answered breathlessly. "I can scarce believe it. He actually spoke to me.''

"A few words from his lips can seal or ruin one's social success, although,'' she added, eyeing Jacey curiously, "it can scarce matter to *you*.''

Jacey looked up at her again. "Indeed? Why not?''

"You are to be married soon, as I am.''

At last Jacey realised to whom she was speaking. Lady Griselda Dunscombe, the daughter of this evening's host and hostess.

"Yes, I know. You are betrothed to the Duke of Ormesby.''

The girl smiled. "And you to Lord Sheringham. A secret, romantic attachment, if the tattle-baskets are to be believed.''

Her tone indicated her readiness not to believe it. Jacey did not comment and the girl added, "We have a deal in common, Miss Trevallion."

Silently Jacey doubted it, but smiled nonetheless.

"You must be in high dudgeon," Lady Griselda went on, "because Sheringham has not arrived."

The reminder caused Jacey to feel light-hearted once again. "On the contrary, I am enjoying a delightful miscellany of dancing partners in his stead."

Lady Griselda looked even more mystified. "I assure you I should not countenance such heedless behaviour from Ormesby."

"In that you are perfectly correct, Lady Griselda. It would appear that I am exceeding foolhardy."

Lady Griselda continued to gaze at her curiously and as the music started up once more, she began to move away, still looking perplexed.

"We must continue this coze on another occasion. I am engaged for the minuet so pray excuse me for now."

After the girl had gone Jacey chuckled at her dismay, and then became aware of more eyes upon her. A dozen gentlemen and a like number of ladies were quizzing her.

The noise all around her was loud and the room overbearingly hot. She was suddenly afflicted with a desire to be alone, to reflect upon her encounter with the famous Beau Brummel, but even as she fled the ballroom she was aware it was because she feared that any one of the roués eyeing her with interest could just be the Earl of Sheringham who might have arrived at that moment. The thought caused her to shiver uncontrollably and the urge to flee became even greater.

Seven

Miss Trevallion was well-occupied in her rubber of whist and as her niece wandered through the card room she did not even raise her head.

Jacey noticed that guests were still arriving which caused her to be slightly uneasy, but she did think it possible that the Earl of Sheringham was out of Town at present. Even though her curiosity about him was great, her fear of meeting him was even more so, and any postponement of the evil day was welcome. In the meantime she vowed to work hard to encourage Lady Moncourt's pursuit of Sir John.

After a while she wandered out on to one of the balconies which overlooked a garden. Jacey was glad not to find anyone else there, although noises from the shrubbery indicated that several people were seeking their entertainment in the garden.

The air was welcomingly fresh although she knew her aunt would be scandalised to find her there with no shawl to keep her warm. She would, no doubt, predict any number of dangerous illnesses which could be contracted from such rash behaviour.

She reflected that her first society ball had been a great success. Everyone she had met had been all amiability, but she couldn't help wondering what life would be like as a married woman. It would all depend upon Lord Sheringham and how he was likely to treat her. Because she did not wish to dwell upon such thoughts she quickly diverted her mind instead towards Beau Brummel who had condescended to speak to her. It was no wonder he had become the prime arbiter of fashion; his style was quite remarkable and it was obvious many gentlemen had set out to emulate him, with less success, however. Her own Papa was most elegantly dressed, too, as was the charming Mr. Pringle.

Jacey could not help but admire *his* style, too. He had been so insistent in his attentions, making no attempt to disguise his admiration of her. Jacey's body quivered with pleasure at the thought of it. Geoffrey Pringle. He had no title – at least as yet – but to be invited to the Dunscombe's ball meant he must be well-connected. Perhaps he was wealthy, she mused. Rich enough even to be willing to pay Papa's debts to gain a bride ...

When the window on to the balcony began to open she did not wait to see who it was; she ran down the steps and into the garden itself. Although she was enjoying the ball immensely and was engaged for several more sets she did relish this opportunity for solitude, to reflect upon all which had happened. In Cornwall solitude had been her companion for so long the habit could not be dismissed entirely.

She fled as far as a folly where the music could be heard less clearly. It had been built in the form of a circular Greek temple. It was evidently delightful on a fine summer day, but suddenly she shivered slightly in the breeze and knew she must go back.

As she turned on her heel a voice out of the darkness

startled her. "It must be a dream. Such a divine vision cannot be real."

Jacey drew back for fear of intruding upon some rendezvous but then she caught sight of someone in the shadows of the temple and gasped with alarm. It was then that she realised the comment had been addressed to her.

Recovering her composure she answered, "I thank you, sir, but I am indeed human."

She made to go past him but he came forward then and she could see he was a fairly young man of above average height with a fine figure on which his evening coat and satin breeches sat well. His eyes seemed to burn darkly and his curls were slightly windswept. As he came closer to her Jacey realised that he was also slightly the worse for drink and she drew further away, back into the centre of the temple.

"My old nurse used to tell me of fairies to be found at the bottom of every garden. I can tell her there is a Greek goddess in this one and surely you would not wish to prove me wrong."

Sensible now that it had been foolhardy of her to venture so far from the house alone, Jacey began to be alarmed. It was well known that many bucks forgot their manners after a few glasses of champagne.

"Please excuse me, sir."

Once again she made to go past him, but he placed himself foursquare in the way. Alarm made her quiver again as he said in a low voice, thickened by an excess of alcohol, "I cannot credit you will disappoint me. If I allow you to flee I fear you will disappear for ever."

She looked up into his face. A pair of dark eyes burned intently into hers. Jacey's breath caught in her throat.

"I beg of you allow me to go, sir."

He made no move to allow her past and Jacey, studied him more closely. There was a moon in a cloudless sky and by the light of it she was able to recognise his mocking expression. His lips were curved into a travesty of a satyr's smile. There was something unreal about him, too, just at that moment.

Then, she realised, she had seen him somewhere before, although she could not recall a meeting. Suddenly she gasped again.

"I have seen you on another occasion. In the Park yesterday – with ... Mollie Dinsdale."

"How remarkably observant of you. If I recall correctly you were accompanied by Sir John Trevallion." His smile appeared to be a cruel one just then. "Sir John Trevallion," he repeated contemptuously. "That old scapegrace is past praying for. A pretty pair you make, but let me tell you he'll not buy you the pretty gee-gaws you crave, my dear, whatever he promises, although I admire his insolence in bringing you here. How did he present you to old Dunscombe? He is bold enough to call you his lightskirt in public."

"You are mad as well as foxed, sir!" she gasped, turning on her heel.

"Don't turn away from me."

He reached out for her and drew her close, looking down into her startled face. It was clear he intended to kiss her and outraged she drew away yet again, aware of his assumption of her morals.

"This is outside of enough! I am Sir John Trevallion's daughter."

A look of alarm crossed the man's face to her satisfaction. As she was about to flee his unwanted embrace he caught hold of her again, staring at her in the moonlight. She had the distinct impression he had become suddenly sober.

"By gad, so you are."

Attempting to control her anger and alarm Jacey said calmly, "Pray allow me to leave or else I shall be obliged to inform my father of your unspeakable behaviour."

He ignored her dire threat and repeated, "So you are Trevallion's daughter."

Unexpectedly he began to laugh and Jacey began to be convinced she was trapped by a lunatic.

His laughter faded but there was still a devilish gleam in his eyes. "I shall have my kiss in any event."

He pulled her close and before she could protest further had pressed his lips roughly on to hers. Outraged Jacey could only struggle in vain, for his strength held her an easy captive. After a moment or two she no longer fought to free herself as an unfamiliar emotion assailed her senses. It was not an unpleasant one.

At last he released her, laughing again. She stared at him, realising he was laughing at her passionate response. She was herself shocked by the unexpectedness of it. She had been led to believe such assaults were horrid and yet she had enjoyed his embrace thoroughly.

She continued to stare at him in horror for a moment or two before turning on her heel and running headlong back towards the house.

In her panic to escape him she had, however, taken the wrong direction, and after a while she was so breathless that she was forced to risk being discovered by her unknown assailant and sank down wearily into a garden seat. Her lips still tingled from his kiss and her heart beat unevenly. Even though the evening breeze was a cool one her cheeks felt hot and she put her hands to them.

Eventually her harsh breathing returned to its normal pace and it was then that she realised she could no longer hear any music, although she could see the lighted windows of the house through the trees.

Straightening the folds of her gown she then made her more sedate way back through the garden although she was still fearful of encountering that man again. Fortunately she reached the house with no further mishap and a glance in one of the mirrors assured her she looked none the worse for her encounter.

Almost immediately she was approached by Geoffrey Pringle and for some reason she looked at him anew. Aware of it he gave her a quizzical glance and she became flustered yet again.

"Miss Trevallion, I have been seeking you everywhere."

"I needed to take the air, Mr. Pringle."

"You must have a care not to catch a chill, and you should not in any event venture out alone. It is most foolhardy."

"You are full of good sense."

"I do hope I may prevail upon you to allow me to take you to supper."

Jacey stared at him wide-eyed as if she had never seen him before. All at once she wondered whether a kiss from his lips would provoke a similar response in her, and as if to obliterate the treacherous thought closed her eyes.

"Miss Trevallion."

"I should be pleased," she answered with deceptive calm, aware that he was regarding her curiously.

The supper room was crowded as might be expected. Out of the corner of her eye Jacey caught sight of Lady Moncourt and Sir John, which pleased her, and mercifully no sign of the man from the garden.

When they had chosen their repast from the ample buffet. Mr. Pringle found seats in a corner and set about eating a hearty supper. Jacey could only watch and admire him, for her own appetite had disappeared entirely.

"Are you not hungry, Miss Trevallion?" he asked at last.

She smiled wanly. "Apparently not."

"I cannot conceive why I eat so heartily, for I have only just heard the most appalling news."

She stiffened with alarm. "Oh dear. What can it be? Not Bonaparte …?"

"As far as I am aware he remains at the other side of the Channel. However, it distresses me to learn that you, Miss Trevallion, are already betrothed and soon to be wed."

She cast him a weak smile. "That is so, and within a month."

"I am totally devastated. So soon. You have only just arrived in Town. How can it be? But, of course, it is quite understandable. Sheringham has superb taste. I have always admired it in him and never more so than now."

Her cheeks grew pink as she averted her face.

"I cannot, however, admire his neglect of you this evening."

"Lord Sheringham must have been delayed

unexpectedly.''

"Indeed he has been here some time to my knowledge.''

Jacey stared at him uncomprehendingly. "You must be mistaken, Mr. Pringle.''

"Indeed not. He was only a short while ago staring at us quite fiercely from across the room, but I declare it is the consquence of his own folly which results in your being attended by another.''

She glanced around almost fearfully to where he had indicated. An elderly dandy was eyeing her through his quizzing glass and she ventured, "Do you still see him, Mr. Pringle?''

The young man glanced around and to her relief declared, "He must have left the room. I should also be bursting with envy in his place. He will just be obliged to make certain he arrives in good time on another occasion, although I dare to hope that my own humble companionship has not been too onerous in his absence.''

"On the contrary, Mr. Pringle, it is exceeding convivial.''

He seemed gratified by her response and putting down his empty plate he took her full one. "If you don't wish to eat, may I escort you back to the ballroom? The minuet is mine, I think, and the sets are being made up.''

As they went back into the ballroom, Jacey's mind was in a whirl. The evening's events had all but overwhelmed her and she knew now it would be a relief when it was over.

She had only just finished dancing with Mr. Pringle when she saw Sir John approaching through the crowds. "If you wish to engage me for a dance, Papa, you are too late," she told him pertly.

He took her arm and pulled her to one side, behind a marble pillar. All at once she noted he was less than pleased which she immediately associated with the earl.

"Papa, why did you not tell me Sheringham is here?"

"I didn't know he was," he answered irritably. "Did you or did you not tell Lady Moncourt about the matter of your marriage?"

"I informed her of my betrothal but certainly not all the relevant details of how it came about. Why are you in such a pucker about it?"

He sucked in his breath. "The impudent hussy has just offered me a loan to get me out of any scrape I might be in."

At this news her demeanour brightened. "Impudent? I declare it is most handsome of her. Can you not accept, Papa?"

"Of course I cannot! Can you imagine being in debt to Lady Moncourt? How could I repay her?"

Jacey shrugged. "At least I should not be obliged to marry *her*."

His face grew red and she was immediately sorry she had spoken.

"I beg your pardon if you are displeased, Papa."

He smiled at last to her relief. "I cannot be displeased with you for very long. I really do appreciate how sporting you've been about all this. I'm not proud of myself, I can tell you, and it's deuced awkward about Maria. Incidentally I cannot imagine where you've gained this bad impression of Sheringham. He's not such a bad fellow, Jacey."

"I shall judge better on that score when I finally

meet him, although I am beginning to believe I am not meant to do so."

One of his eyebrows rose a fraction. "What an odd notion!"

"For all I know he may be a crook-back."

Sir John laughed. "I cannot conceive who has given you these odd notions. Ah, let me guess. M'sister, eh? For ever Friday-faced. Full of megrims."

It was Jacey's turn to laugh then. "No, Papa. You do her a great injustice. But what am I to think?"

"I am only surprised you display such eagerness to make his acquaintance if you are so pessimistic about the fellow."

"I am far from eager, merely anxious to see what I am about to take on."

"Would I allow you to marry anyone too frightful?" he teased.

"Yes, considering the alternative."

"Don't think I haven't pondered upon it, my lovely, because I have, and I am persuaded Sheringham will make a good husband. Yes, I am sure of it. Nothing less than a congenial marriage would do for you."

He gave her his arm and they strolled back into the ballroom. He patted her hand encouragingly. "Don't you fret now, my lovely. I can deal with Maria Moncourt."

"All you need to do is refuse her generosity. It cannot be difficult for you."

She cast him an ironic look which discomforted him and then she asked, "Papa, do you recall seeing a Mollie Dinsdale in that curricle yesterday?"

"Er ... yes ... why?"

"I wanted to ask if you knew who was dri ..."

Her question faded somewhat abruptly as did her

smile, for coming towards them was the Marchioness of Moncourt clinging to the arm of none other than the man from the garden.

Once again his lips were curved into that satyr's smile and Jacey turned as if to run away, only it was not quite so easy now.

"We have been seeking you everywhere," Lady Moncourt declared. "You are devilishly difficult to find."

Sir John looked acutely discomforted but the reason why was only evident a moment later when the marchioness said, "Miss Trevallion, my dear, only see who is here. Sheringham, is it not time you stood up for at least one set with your bride-to-be?"

Jacey's eyes opened wide with horror as he bowed before her. "Miss Trevallion, your servant."

The room seemed to whirl around Jacey's head, but all the while she was aware of his mocking smile and alarm of those around her.

"Catch her, Trevallion," she heard someone say. "She is going to swoon."

It sounded like the voice of Lord Sheringham himself.

"It has all been too much for her," said Lady Moncourt worriedly.

"Where is my vinaigrette?" That was Aunt Minerva.

"You had better take her home."

Surely that couldn't be Lord Sheringham again.

Of all people, not him, she thought through the clouds of mist which surrounded her.

"Awful ... never swooned before in her life ... all your fault, Trevallion. London air is putrid ... all manner of ills ..."

"Here let me help you, Trevallion."

That was Lord Sheringham again.

"I need no help from you, I thank you."

Jacey felt herself being borne through the air and then mercifully they all went away, leaving oblivion in their place.

Eight

"The Lord be praised."

Jacey blinked and saw Aunt Minerva bending over her. She realised then that she was in her own bed and bewilderedly looked about her, seeking to recall the reason for her incapacity.

"What am I doing here?"

"You swooned at the Dunscombe's ball and then lapsed into a fever, no doubt because someone opened a window. To give you air indeed! Congestion of the lungs, more like."

Jacey's head swam. "I am never ill, Aunt."

"I am delighted to hear you say so," Miss Trevallion answered wryly. "We shall consider this occasion an oversight. I shall never forgive your Papa for allowing you to meet Lord Sheringham for the first time in such a shocking way. It was enough to overset the stoutest nerves."

Jacey didn't trouble to tell her aunt it had not been the first meeting.

"When did this happen?"

"Two nights ago."

Jacey was aghast. "So long! I cannot credit it."

"You have been quite ill. We've all been so concerned for you. Doctor Chetwynd came to bleed you yesterday." As Jacey peered down at the plaster on her arm her aunt went on, "I feared the brain fever, and told Doctor Chetwynd so."

"I trust the doctor was good enough to abide by your superior knowledge, Aunt."

Miss Trevallion flushed. "Tush. Even now you insist upon roasting me." She smiled then. "Only see all the flowers, Jacey."

For the first time Jacey did glance around the room and saw the profusion of flowers all around her. Baskets, posies and bouquets were everywhere. Miss Trevallion busied herself walking around the room.

"This one is from your Papa, Lady Moncourt – such exquisite taste – the Dunscombes, of course. They were mortified that you should be taken ill at *their* ball. These are from a Mr. Pringle; I have no notion who he might be. Oh, and naturally, Sheringham, too," she added, indicating the largest. "Moreover, you will be gratified to learn that he has called in on several occasions during the time of your illness."

Jacey was scarcely that. Again her cheeks grew pink at the very thought of meeting him again. "Well, I don't wish to see him."

Aunt Minerva raised her eyebrows. "As you wish, my dear, but you will have to see him some time."

"On the day of the wedding will be soon enough."

Miss Trevallion peered at her keenly. "The fever has left you peevish, which is only to be expected. Once you have some sustenance you will feel much better."

Jacey sank back into the pillows. "I cannot face a morsel."

"Indeed, and a heavy meal would not be at all

advisible. However, I have made you some beef tea."
She came back towards the bed with the dish. "Here
let me feed it to you."

Jacey did not demur, for she knew it would be futile
to do so. Miss Trevallion seated herself by the bed and
began to feed her niece.

"I confess, my dear, Lord Sheringham recomm-
ended himself to me most highly. I found him to
be a pleasant young man, and not at all what I had
envisaged. It was a great relief."

Jacey almost choked on the beef tea. "Oh, Aunt,
how can you judge on so short an acquaintance?"

Her aunt bridled. "I have always deemed myself a
good judge of character. His manners are very pretty
and his concern for you at the ball — something of
which you cannot be aware — was handsome.
Moreover, I am persuaded you will admit his looks are
quite tolerable, and such matters are of the greatest
import to young girls."

"He is a dissipated rake of abominable moral
fibre."

Miss Trevallion looked amused. "I do not doubt it."

"Then how can you praise him so?"

"Did you truly expect him to be a paragon of virtue,
dear? I declare that would have been too much."

Jacey turned away in disgust and her aunt put the
empty dish to one side. Just then the door opened and
Sir John put his head around the crack.

"Ah, awake at last, and looking so much better.
You gave us all quite a fright, my lovely."

"I feel much improved, Papa," and then, as he was
about to come into the room she added, "but I would
like to be left alone just now."

His expression gave way to one of dismay. "Could

you not spare a few moments of your time for Lady Moncourt? She has been waiting downstairs for an age."

Jacey immediately brightened. "Of course. Have her shown up."

A few minutes later Lady Moncourt hurried into the room, bearing a box of marchpane which she deposited on the counterpane.

"How glad I am to see you so much recovered!"

Miss Trevallion vacated her chair for Lady Moncourt who, after kissing Jacey on the brow sat down.

"I will stay only a few minutes. Trevallion tells me you still remain peevish."

Jacey laughed. "Not with you, Lady Moncourt. Do you not feel men are the very devil?"

The marchioness laughed delightedly. "Oh, my dear, I do, very often, but at your age you should not."

She eyed her sombrely for a moment or two before saying, "You must take life a little more easily from now on, my dear. It is little more than three weeks to your wedding and you would not wish to go to your bridegroom hollow-eyed."

"If I die instead perchance it will solve the problem nicely."

Lady Moncourt clucked her tongue as Miss Trevallion said, "How wicked!"

"I fear she is still peevish, as Trevallion observed. Really, my dear, you should consider yourself fortunate. The Earl of Sheringham has been the object of matrimonial interest for years. There are many who would consider themselves most fortunate to attract his interest, let alone an offer of marriage."

"He didn't – offer, I mean."

"Trevallion leads me to believe that he did."

"Then he offered for my portion."

"That is nothing out of the common, you know."

Jacey sighed. "Yes, I do know, Lady Moncourt."

"I did make an attempt to help, but Trevallion is as proud as the Devil, and I can only admire it in him."

Once again a sigh escaped Jacey. "I know, and I am not unappreciative, Lady Moncourt."

"I only wish I could be of true help, although being wed to Sheringham is not the worse thing I can think of. Indeed there are those who would consider it wonderful."

She laughed, but on not eliciting any amusement from the invalid went on, "La! here am I, prattling on like an addle-pate. I called only to ascertain your well being."

"You need harbour no concerns on my behalf, Lady Moncourt. I will contrive handsomely."

The marchioness did not look convinced but she went on to say, "When you are recovered fully you must visit Jenkin's Emporium in the Strand and choose some material for your wedding gown. I am well-known there so there will be no problem, and my mantua-maker will be only too delighted to make it up for you. She is Madame Fleur and you will find her in Bond Street. I do trust that you won't be too proud to go."

She looked anxiously at Jacey whose eyes suddenly filled with tears. "I would not, for anything, refuse your kindness, my lady."

The marchioness patted her hand and then got to her feet. "By the by, Sheringham is waiting downstairs. I do not suppose you wish to see him."

Jacey's eyes grew wide with alarm as she cried, "No! Indeed, I do not!"

* * *

"I was to have had cream satin," Miss Trevallion mused as she fingered the material put out for their consideration, "but I dare say silver lace will suit you the better."

Jacey scarcely glanced at it before saying irritably, "Whoever has heard of a silver-lace shroud?"

"Jacey! These dramatics are unbecoming a well-brought up young lady."

"I beg your pardon, Aunt." She glanced at the mercer's assistant. "Yes, the silver-lace will do."

Miss Trevallion sighed with relief before saying in a low voice, "Really, Jacey, when you believed Lord Sheringham to be an old and gouty man you were less reluctant to become his wife than now when he is known to be a perfectly presentable young man, and not without means either. You are to be congratulated rather than pitied."

"Yes, I do know, and I am glad he has found favour with you."

"I am heartily relieved on your behalf. Moreover, since you were ill he has called a dozen times to my knowledge, and the pity is you will not receive him. That is what I call shabby of you, Jacey."

"When we resume our social visiting, Aunt, I dare say we shall encounter Lord Sheringham at every turn."

Even as she spoke Jacey dreaded the possibility. She felt she could never face him, nor could she forgive him mistaking her for a light-skirt. The very recollection of his kiss caused her cheeks to redden.

"The purchase of the material is a great relief," Miss Trevallion was saying. "It is handsome of Lady Moncourt to make a gift to you."

"Papa is a chucklehead not to marry her."

"There is nothing to say she would accept even if he did come up to scratch."

"I'll warrant that she would."

Miss Trevallion drew a sigh. "It is not like to happen. The Trevallions have always been proud, my dear, and you have no less inherited the trait."

"We really cannot afford the luxury of pride."

Jacey's aunt chuckled. "Not being able to afford something is not usually a bar to having it in our family."

Jacey drew on her gloves and was unaware of anything untoward until her aunt said, "Good day to you, my lord. It is unusual to find a gentleman in a mercer's emporium."

Jacey froze and looked up hesitantly as if fearing what she might see. Sure enough Lord Sheringham was coming across the shop floor towards them. She stiffened with shock and was further surprised to find her aunt smiling as foolishly as any green girl.

The earl, on this occasion, was not smiling, nor did his expression mock. He looked to be quite grim as he removed his curly-brimmed beaver and nodded to them both.

"Good day to you, ladies. I trust you, Miss Trevallion, have recovered your health."

Jacey straightened up. "Yes, I thank you, my lord."

"I happened to be passing when I caught sight of Sir John's carriage and deemed it opportune to pay my respects."

"And we couldn't be more delighted that you did. Could we, Jacey?" Miss Trevallion cast her niece a warning look.

Jacey contrived to smile. "It is good in Lord Sheringham to spare us the time."

"You may not be aware of it, but my time has been somewhat at your disposal of late." A comment which caused Jacey to shift uncomfortably.

"I don't suppose you will be surprised to learn we have been purchasing material for Jacey's wedding gown," Miss Trevallion told him in an unusually coy tone which caused Jacey to draw in an irate breath.

The earl smiled uncertainly in response. "It is fortunate I did not arrive five minutes ago. That wouldn't have done at all."

"Oh, you would not have been allowed to see it, you may be sure. Not even a glance, Lord Sheringham."

She cast Jacey a reproachful glance, no doubt because of her icy silence. However at last the earl did look directly at Jacey again and she was forced to avert her eyes.

"Miss Trevallion, would you accord me the honour of driving you home?"

Before she could turn down the offer her aunt said, "What a splendid notion! I have several more calls to make, and my niece is noticeably weary. She is not fully recovered from her illness. Illness is so prevalent in London, is it not?"

"I believe the cold night air is most harmful, Miss Trevallion."

Jacey noticed then that there was a mischievous gleam in his eye and was moved to answer, "I am quite, quite well now, I thank you, and I'd as lief return in my father's carriage when you have completed your shopping, Aunt."

"Nonsense," her aunt argued, smiling placatingly at the earl. "You must not concern yourself with me. I shall contrive well enough. Off you go."

Maddening as Aunt Minerva often could be, it was the first time Jacey felt she could have enjoyed strangling her. However, without a further word she walked with the earl out of the emporium and to the very curricle she had seen him in on that first occasion.

On seeing it she hesitated, recalling that Mollie Dinsdale had been the passenger on that occasion.

As he handed her up she couldn't help remarking, "I feel that a bird of quite a different plumage is more suited to this seat."

"Some birds have colourful plumage, others have sharp claws," he answered to her annoyance as his tiger climbed up behind and the earl took the ribbons.

They rode along in silence for a while and she was rather surprised that he made no attempt at conversation. After a while it became rather irksome. Every now and again she cast him a sideways glance but he seemed not to notice.

At length she was forced to say, "Lord Sheringham, I am as yet unfamiliar with London, but I feel we are not on our way to Bedford Square."

As if in answer the curricle drew into the side of the very quiet road along which they had been travelling. He put down the ribbons and turned to her, causing her to flinch away in alarm. He didn't miss the gesture and it made him smile faintly.

"You need have no fear, Miss Trevallion, I shall not cause you any further outrage. I wish only to talk with you."

She glanced at the tiger perched behind them and, guessing her thoughts, he added, "Wilkins is the soul of discretion."

At this comment she could not help but smile. "I dare say he would need to be."

"You have not resided in London for long as yet, and you still remain unused to Town life."

Miffed Jacey answered, "If you mean that I am a green girl, I readily acknowledge the fact, and I shall not beg your pardon for it."

"I trust that you will not. However, I have called at your father's house on several occasions and you have been unavailable every time. It is, therefore, unavoidable that we talk here before I return you home."

Giving him a suspicious look she asked, "What would you wish to talk about?"

He considered the top of his riding whip carefully. "First of all I would wish to beg your pardon for my behaviour at Lord Dunscombe's ball. Had I known ..."

She stiffened at the reminder of that awful episode. "It is evident that you did not. You believed me to be a person of a different character."

He made no attempt to hide his irritation. "You are remarkable magnanimous, but I fear you still do not forgive me."

"You were foxed."

"That is no excuse, but I trust you will find it in your heart to grant me forgiveness."

His humility was confusing, for it seemed a little out of character. Whilst she did not doubt his sincerity on this occasion, she took leave to doubt he would not assault some other female in a like manner when the feeling came over him.

"I do understand that gentlemen behave on occasions in such a manner."

As he considered her he smiled faintly. "Your generosity overwhelms me, ma'am."

She turned to give him a sharp look, convinced that his manner mocked her, but his answering gaze was so bland she was forced to look away again in confusion.

"Now we have set matters to rights, mayhap you will return me to Bedford Square."

"Although it was my intention to beg your pardon at the earliest moment, that is not in fact what I wish to discuss with you." Once again she turned to look at him as he went on in a soft voice, "It would be foolish for us not to talk of the circumstances of our betrothal. The wedding is not far away."

Jacey almost flinched to hear him speak of it. Until that moment the spectre was not real.

"You and Papa have already discussed it sufficiently, I feel."

"Miss Trevallion, you are being most provoking."

"That was not my intention."

"You have not as yet given your opinion on the matter."

"That is because my opinion is of no consequence."

"It most certainly is to me!" After a moment he said in a less heated manner, "What I wish to ascertain is that you agree with the arrangements which have been made."

Her head snapped up. "Do I have a choice, Lord Sheringham?"

"Indeed you do."

"How can that be? If I do not marry you my father will be incarcerated in a debtor's jail."

It was his turn to look away. "He gave me an assurance you were willing to embark upon this marriage."

"And so I am."

"You must forgive me if I take leave to doubt it. Your attitude is positively hostile. You show no appreciation of my good nature in agreeing to the scheme."

"Your good nature …!"

Her voice died away for she was suddenly afraid of offending him. If he were to cry off, it would be disastrous.

"If I have given you cause to doubt me, then it is my turn to beg your pardon."

Her words were accompanied by a beseeching look, but all the while she hated to be in so invidious a position. It was totally alien to her true nature and she had the feeling that he was well aware of it.

"You have no need to apologise, I assure you. Only tell me you do indeed wish to proceed and I shall be satisfied."

"I … do."

She could no longer look at him, but she knew he was regarding her carefully. It was an unnerving experience, for she felt he could discern her true thoughts in the matter.

"Very well," he said at last, to her profound relief. "I am satisfied. The wedding, I understand, is to be on the twenty-third of next month."

Alarmed anew she gasped, "I … didn't know it was actually arranged."

His lips quirked into a smile. "Sir John is more than

a little anxious that I don't change my mind."

Angered once again she retorted, "Is there a possibility of your doing so?"

He looked outraged. "Miss Trevallion, I have given my word; the bargain is agreed upon."

"Bargain," she echoed in dismay. "How cold you make it sound."

His eyes narrowed somewhat. "You must surely be aware that financial considerations are at the root of most marriages."

Her face was a picture of the deepest despair. "So I am coming to understand, but I had never thought that such a consideration would apply to me."

"Neither had I," he answered emphatically. "I assure you it was not my doing."

"I cannot find it in my heart to blame Papa," she answered quietly, almost to herself, "although I do feel you could marry to greater advantage elsewhere."

She held her breath expectantly as he answered, laughingly, "Oh, indeed I could, Miss Trevallion, but how else can I collect what I am owed? It is no small sum and I have no mind to forgo it, so be assured that I shall not cry off unless the direst circumstances call upon me to do so. I am a man of honour and you may rely upon my word."

"My father is also a man of honour," she snapped.

He continued to smile which made her long to snatch up his riding whip and lash out at him with it. That she did not was a miracle of self-control.

To her relief he took up the ribbons again and the curricle moved off. Their conversation had in no way reassured her of the future, for she had come close to disliking him even more than before.

It was to her great relief that the curricle moved into

Bedford Square. Their conversation had gained little save the knowledge that his distaste for this marriage was as great as hers. It did not augur well for the future, although she supposed he would go his own way for most of the time, which was a small relief.

When the carriage came to a halt outside the house he jumped down almost before his servant did. He immediately offered her his hand although she hesitated to take it for a moment. Her reluctance seemed to amuse him anew and she accepted his hand. Then when she had climbed down she relinquished his hold immediately, making a great business of adjusting her pelisse.

Aware that he was watching her and had made no move to go she looked up sharply. Suddenly her cheeks began to redden beneath his scrutiny.

"You really shouldn't scowl so," he told her in a chiding tone.

Immediately Jacey stiffened. "I was never used to in Cornwall, I assure you."

To her chagrin he laughed. "This is all a sore trial to you, is it not, Miss Trevallion?"

"Naturally, Lord Sheringham. I dare say it is even more so to you."

"In that event we should both try to like each other the better. Time is passing."

She shuddered at the reminder. At last he moved away from her.

"Lord Sheringham," she said quickly, "if my father does raise enough money to pay off his debt to you before the twenty-third of next month would you be willing to call off this wedding?"

He halted in his tracks and when he turned to her again he looked surprised.

"I understand that there is no question of his being able to do so, that all possible ways had been explored. I allowed him a deal of time."

"Yes, yes, I am aware of his difficulty, but if it were possible what would you say?"

"That would depend upon you, Miss Trevallion."

She could not help but laugh, albeit rather harshly. "You may assume that I would be willing to cry off."

"It would be devilishly awkward once the announcement was made."

"It is not uncommon for one or other of the parties to cry off a marriage."

He smiled with unexpected naturalness. "But which one of us shall be the jilt?"

Jacey bit back a cry of exasperation. She was quite convinced that he was deliberately provoking her to anger — and enjoying the experience — but she remained determined not to allow him to succeed.

"If it concerns your pride, my lord, you may consider me the jilt. I do not care for such matters."

"You should. It may well affect your future prospects. Gentlemen are notoriously reluctant to pay court to a jilt, Miss Trevallion, even one who is confoundedly pretty."

Her cheeks flamed. "As if I care! My aunt declares that a portion is all the allure a woman needs."

"Allow me to inform you it is not."

With her cheeks growing even redder Jacey asked in exasperation, "Will you be pleased to answer my question, Lord Sheringham?"

"By all means." Suddenly the gleam of amusement died from his eyes to be replaced by a steely look. "Needless to say, if the debt is paid there can be nothing more to do."

Jacey drew in a deep sigh of relief and was about to go into the house when he added, "However, Miss Trevallion, do not seek to gammon me in this matter. You may imagine I am not up to snuff, but I assure you that I am not easily tricked."

Breathlessly, she answered, "I would not dream of doing so, Lord Sheringham."

He smiled again as he tipped his hat to her. "You relieve me, Miss Trevallion, for I have waited an unconscionable time for settlement of my account, and I would truly dislike seeing Sir John in the Fleet."

Stunned at the implied threat she watched him climb into the coachman's seat and flicking his whip over the backs of his horses, he drove off with no further glance in her direction.

Nine

"Every day brings us more invitations," Miss Trevallion said gleefully over breakfast a few days after Jacey's ride with Lord Sheringham.

Since then she had encountered him at every turn, much to her chagrin, and she was beginning to fear, for the first time since arriving in London, that she might actually be obliged to go ahead with the marriage after all.

Common sense told her that Lady Moncourt and Sir John were not going to announce their betrothal before that – if ever. Their easy-going relationship had gone on too long, and it was never likely that he would acquire enough wealth to feel able to offer her marriage.

Every day Jacey awoke to a deeper feeling of apprehension, for she could now see no other way out of the morass.

She eyed her aunt resentfully. "You was never used to enjoy social diversions, Aunt."

Miss Trevallion gave one of her rare laughs as she put down the handful of invitations next to her breakfast plate. "My dear, my last visit to Town was on my own come-out Season and you know how that ended. This time I can sit back and enjoy myself."

"I only wish that I could."

"Jacey, you should. You should be in high snuff. Life could not be better for you."

Jacey did not deign to reply. Morosely she took a morsel of food on to her fork before lifting up the posy of flowers she had by her plate.

"Are those not Lord Sheringham's flowers?" Miss Trevallion asked in an uncharacteristically coy voice.

"No, Aunt Minerva, these are not. This posy is from Mr. Pringle. I dare say you are acquainted with him."

Miss Trevallion did not look pleased. "That young man is remarkable persistent in view of the fact you will be a bride in three weeks' time."

"He is indeed," Jacey answered in delight. "Not a day passes by without some gee-gaw from him arriving. Of course, he is not alone. I do have other admirers."

"But none who pleases you as much as Mr. Pringle."

"Few others have such a pleasing manner, Aunt."

Miss Trevallion looked even less pleased. "I take leave to disagree."

"Do you think that Mr. Pringle might be wealthy, Aunt Minerva?"

"I couldn't possibly say. He looks exceeding poor to me."

Jacey sighed. "That was my understanding."

Her aunt's eyes narrowed. "I was quite certain that Lord Sheringham had sent flowers today."

Jacey began to eat more heartily now. "He did. They are on the table in the hall."

Miss Trevallion leaned across the table. "My dear girl, I cannot conceive why you have taken Lord Sheringham in so much dislike."

"He is far too top-lofty for my taste, Aunt."

"I can assure you that you are the envy of this year's debutantes, and those of several years past."

"They are all welcome to him, I assure you," she answered airily. Her aunt made an impatient sound and Jacey went on, "You cannot expect me to exhibit any enthusiasm for a man of his ilk."

"I really cannot conceive what you may mean by that. I find him quite charming."

"How blind you must be, Aunt Minerva; he is vain and arrogant, and those are the least of his faults."

"Well, I find him all amiability. It is quite crack-brained of you to favour Mr. Pringle. His tongue is well-hung, I grant you, but that is all."

"'Tis enough."

There was a pause before Miss Trevallion said in a cajoling voice, "I have just thought that there is like to be seven duchesses at your wedding."

"And one earl too many," Jacey answered darkly.

The door burst open just then, much to Miss Trevallion's relief and admitted Sir John, who was waving his copy of the *Gazette* in the air.

"Here it is, my lovely! The official announcement of your forthcoming nuptials."

Jacey groaned and her aunt said, in outraged tones, "Betrothed, and treasuring flowers from another man!" Then she went on in a more excited manner, "Oh, do let me see it!"

He handed her the newspaper and immediately went to kiss his daughter on the cheek. "There, my lovely, it is all becoming quite exciting is it not?"

Although his tone was cheery, his eyes lingered worriedly on the flowers.

"Yes, Papa," she answered dutifully, casting him a faint smile.

Miss Trevallion put the newspaper down and brought out her handkerchief. "I am quite overcome," she said tearfully.

Her brother cast her an exasperated look as her chair scraped back. "When are you not, Minerva?"

"You lack simple humanity. My sensibilities are easily overset and you should be glad that you are never afflicted in such a way. Pray do excuse me; I must go to my room. It is all too much for me."

"Let me accompany you, Aunt," Jacey offered but the woman shook her head.

"No, no, there is no need. You stay here with your Papa. You will have a deal to discuss with him, I dare say. I shall be recovered shortly, have no fear."

"Silly old hen," Sir John remarked as the door closed behind her.

Jacey cast him an indulgent look when he seated himself at the table and proceeded to pile his plate with food.

"You really should extend more sympathy to her, Papa."

"It is enough everyone else clucks about her."

"But they do not! That is why we must extend her a mite charity."

"I will bear it in mind."

"You need not gammon me, Papa. I am persuaded you are as devoted to her as she is to you."

He drew a sigh. "I dare say, but she is a trial at times."

"As you are to her and more often, too."

He looked up at her with a devilish smile. "At present you are the only one who troubles my head. Bearing up, eh?"

She nodded, rather than reply and he went on, his

mouth full of eggs, "Knew you'd take a shine to Sheringham. All the girls do, you know. Quite a tongue-pad. I'm beginning to favour the notion of being related to Sheringham myself. There are no establishments which will not grant Sheringham's kinfolk credit."

Jacey gasped with exasperation. "Papa! You will seek no such thing! Give me your word on it. Will you never learn?"

He grinned sheepishly. "You are sadly ignorant of the ways of sophisticated society, my lovely. I have allowed you to rusticate too long."

"If the ways of the *ton* involve being for ever in dun territory I'd as lief remain in Cornwall. Do I have your word?"

He sighed and then growled. "Very well. I shan't do anything to displease you."

Satisfied she began to look through the latest batch of invitations. Some were for functions which would not be held until after her wedding – she did not like the reminder – and she could not be certain of being in London to attend.

Suddenly her hand froze on one of the invitations and her cheeks paled.

"What is it, Jacey?" Sir John asked. "You look as if you've seen a ghost. Don't tell me you're as vapourish as your aunt."

"Indeed I am not! There is a dinner invitation here from the Dowager Countess of Sheringham!"

Her eyes wide with alarm. Sir John, however, only chuckled.

"So the old girl is back in Town, is she? I hardly need to hazard a guess as to why."

"I didn't know Sheringham had a mother!"

"Nonsense; everyone has a mother."

"Alive, I meant," she said in exasperation. "Shall we have to go?"

He laughed. "If we refuse all others, we are obliged to accept this one. One does not refuse an invitation from Fanny Sheringham, my dear."

Jacey's hands flew to her lips. "Do you think she knows the reason why we are to be married?"

"Hardly," he answered with a laugh. "If I recall Lady Sheringham correctly – and I am persuaded that I do – her son, and everyone else, is terrified of her. It would be more than he dares to tell her he is marrying to claim a gaming debt."

Jacey tossed the invitation down on the table. "I shall not be afraid of her. In fact, it will suit me very well if she takes me in dislike."

Sir John stopped eating. "It would not suit me, however."

She smiled in a conciliatory way. "Have no fear, Papa, all will be well. If Lady Sheringham does take me in dislike it will be no doing of mine."

He looked outraged. "How can she possibly not adore you?"

Jacey looked suddenly dispirited. "I might hazard a shrewd guess, Papa."

"Don't let it trouble your head, my lovely."

She cast him a wry look as a footman entered to announce the arrival of the Marchioness of Moncourt.

Sir John seemed taken aback at first and then pleased. "She rises early these days. Show her into the drawing room."

Jacey was already on her feet, dabbing her lips with the napkin. "No doubt she has seen the *Gazette*."

"All London will have seen it, but I trust they won't

all descend upon us."

"Lady Moncourt is a special friend."

He made no comment and when they reached the door Jacey said thoughtfully, "Papa, you have been acquainted with Lady Moncourt for a long time, have you not?"

"Good grief, yes! Years. More than she or I would care to think about."

"And you seem exceeding fond of her."

His cheeks grew red and he cleared his throat noisily before answering, "What kind of a question is that for a girl to ask her father?"

She sighed and went out of the room, not noticing that Sir John had taken Mr. Pringle's posy and had thrown it where it would be taken out with the uneaten food.

Lady Moncourt was already ensconced by the fire in the drawing room.

"For a few minutes I feared I had dragged you from your beds."

"Almost, my dear," Sir John answered laughingly.

Lady Moncourt looked most fetching in a gown and pelisse of green velvet with a matching bonnet braided with silk. Jacey thought her style was out of the common and hoped that her father noticed it.

"I could not wait to be the first to call and wish Miss Trevallion happy."

She held out her hands and Jacey went to place her own in them. As she did so Lady Moncourt searched the girl's face carefully.

"I do hope you are not going to allow your social commitments and the excitement of the coming nuptuals to make you hag-ridden, my dear. I have seen so many brides at the altar looking quite done-up. It does not augur well for a congenial wedding trip." She released Jacey's hands before going on, "I suppose you will be going to Sheringham Hall for yours."

"I have no notion," Jacey replied, moving away quickly so that Lady Moncourt should not see the telling flush creeping up her cheeks.

"Well, it is of no account. Knowing Sheringham as I do it is more like he will wish to remain in London for the rest of the Season. Is it known yet if His Royal Highness will be attending the wedding?"

Jacey turned to her, shocked. "The Prince of Wales?"

Lady Moncourt looked surprised. "Of course! Sheringham is a crony of his, and is for ever at Carlton House. I don't doubt that the Prince will attend unless matters of state prevent him from doing so." Her eyes crinkled in the corners as she smiled. "Although such matters have never interfered with his pursuit of pleasure in the past."

She looked across the room at Sir John, who had seated himself in the corner of the sofa and was engaged in brushing non-existent specks of dust from the arm of his coat.

"Trevallion, you are remarkable silent this morning? Do you have nothing to say to me?"

Sir John subjected her to one of his charming smiles. "My dear Lady Moncourt, when matters of matrimony are to be discussed it is necessary to give ladies their head."

The marchioness cast Jacey another critical look. "I am about to embark upon an expedition to Bond Street. I did wonder if Miss Trevallion would care to accompany me."

Jacey looked immediately intrigued as the prospect was an inviting one. "That is exceeding kind of you, ma'am."

"It is indeed," her father agreed. "My sister is not the most suitable companion for a girl of Jacey's spirits."

"Miss Trevallion contrives admirably," the marchioness told him, "but it does seem to me that in the matter of your daughter's trousseau you are being less than forthcoming. I do trust you appreciate she is in need of suitable clothing to start her off in married life."

"Naturally ... " Sir John began, looking discomforted.

"I would deem it an honour if you would allow me to provide you with a trousseau properly suited to the future Countess of Sheringham," Lady Moncourt told Jacey.

Jacey looked from the marchioness across the room to her father, feeling somewhat bewildered. Sir John's face had grown rather red once more.

"Now look here, Maria, I am perfectly able to provide for my own daughter, I'll have you know."

"No one is more aware of it than I," she answered soothingly, calming his ire in a matter of moments. "'Tis only that Miss Trevallion has no mother to perform this office, and Miss Minerva Trevallion is bedevilled by ill-health and cannot always fulfill the obligation."

Sir John then looked suitably crestfallen. "Beg pardon, Maria. I am persuaded m'daughter will be honoured at your condescension."

Lady Moncourt cast Jacey a knowing smile. "Go along and fetch your outdoor clothes, my dear. I understand that Mitchell's have a consignment of French lace which will not remain in their establishment for long. Do not ask how they came by it, however, for no one will tell you."

Jacey gave her an answering smile as Sir John got to his feet. "You ladies have no need of me, 'tis evident."

"Indeed not," Lady Moncourt agreed. "Go along, Trevallion, as soon as you please. You may leave your daughter in my care."

He took out his watch and shrugged slightly. "Oh, very well. Ladies will insist upon their shopping."

"Only as much as gentlemen will insist upon their gaming and drinking, Trevallion," she answered coyly.

He strode to the door saying, "*Touché*. There is a mill at Spitalfields which I shall attend today and leave you to your own devices."

He bowed to them both and then, exchanging grins with Lady Moncourt, Jacey rushed off to fetch her pelisse and bonnet, filled with admiration at how easily the marchioness could deal with Sir John.

Ten

To Jacey's surprise Lady Moncourt was driving her own phaeton, drawn by a pair of admirable bays; her black page, dressed in full livery, was perched at the back of the carriage.

As he helped Jacey to climb up, Lady Moncourt said, "I am persuaded Sir John's eccentricities and Miss Trevallion's vapours play old Harry with your sensibilities."

Jacey couldn't help but laugh at the truth of the statement, but replied as they set off, "I am exceeding fond of them."

"With good reason, but I do recall all too well the fraught atmosphere when a wedding is about to take place. It is not conducive to taking your ease."

As she spoke, Jacey was looking at her curiously. "Have you been widowed for long, my lady?"

"Too long." She glanced at Jacey momentarily as she negotiated a narrow street. "Tell me, how do you deal with Sheringham now?"

Jacey was forced to look away in dismay. "I am bound to admit not very well."

"My own marriage was arranged." Again Jacey looked at her with interest. "Moncourt was some twenty years my senior, but we dealt well enough together. It is a matter of intent, I feel. In this instance you have an advantage over me; Sheringham is not so old, and I dare say you will deal well enough."

"I do hope you are correct, my lady."

Her tone, however, indicated that she doubted it.

"Your Papa is in many ways a coxcomb, but I do not think he would suffer you to be leg-shackled to a villain."

"You talk a deal of good sense, my lady. In any event I am obliged to you for taking me up in this way."

"Tush!" was her reply as she flicked the whip over the backs of her team.

Jacey was full of admiration, for she handled the horses as well as any man.

"We are invited to Lady Sheringham's for dinner," she confided a few moments later, sounding dispirited once more.

"No doubt that will be on the same evening I am to be there."

At this news Jacey's demeanour immediately brightened. "That would be altogether wonderful. It will be good to have at least one friend present."

Lady Moncourt chuckled. "My dear, it will not be such an ordeal, and I dare say there will be any number of acquaintances present."

"Do you know Lady Sheringham?"

The marchioness laughed again and at the same time someone in a passing curricle called out to her.

"Do I know Fanny Sheringham? My dear, she is one of my oldest friends. She is some years older than I, but our families were connected and I recall her wedding to Sheringham as if it were yesterday, although I was very small at the time.

"Dear Fanny was not at all suited to her spouse.

The late Lord Sheringham was quite a Corinthian in his day. As a child I admired him immensely. There were times when I believed he would cause Fanny to have apoplexy because of his outrageous behaviour, but I am persuaded they were happy for all that."

They were travelling down Bond Street and the carriage came to a stop outside Mitchell's Haberdashery Emporium. There were a good many elegant carriages awaiting their aristocratic passengers at the roadside, all of them attended by footmen in colourful liveries.

"I have heard tell that Lady Sheringham is somewhat alarming," Jacey ventured as they went inside.

"Now who I wonder has told you such a tale?"

"Papa."

Lady Moncourt nodded sagely. "What a chuckle-head he is! He does nothing for your self-esteem, my dear."

"But is he correct about her?"

"In a way. Fanny Sheringham is full of her own consequence and wonderfully condescending, you may be sure. She will have investigated your ante-cedents thoroughly by now, but I fancy you will not find her too alarming."

Jacey was in no way reassured by this estimation of Lady Sheringham's character, but her mind was soon diverted by the multitude of goods put out for her approval at Mitchell's. Gloves, stockings, shifts, nothing was forgotten, and despite her frequent declarations that there was too much, Lady Moncourt refused to stem the flow of goods put out for them to examine.

"My dear, you will need much more, but by that

time you will be wed and it will be for Sheringham to stump the blunt. I would not deprive him of that pleasure."

After she had given instructions for the goods to be delivered to Bedford Square Lady Moncourt drew on her gloves and eyed Jacey shrewdly.

"Allow me to give you the benefit of my own experience, my dear." When Jacey looked at her with interest, the marchioness went on, sighing slightly, "When one is unhappy I find it useful to put on a cheerful face to the world, for misery always seems greater when others know of it. Moreover, you should, when you are wed, make a style of your own – an outrageous one if need be. Do not allow your unhappiness to be seen and mayhap one day you will discover you are a truly happy person after all."

Jacey gazed at her in awe for a few moments before saying, "Have you ever been unhappy?"

Lady Moncourt laughed delightedly. "Why, certainly, my dear; very often."

"I was never unhappy before."

The marchioness cast her a sympathetic look. "You have endured much since you left your home in Cornwall, but you will soon be settled into your new life, and from all I have seen of you I declare you will enjoy it."

Jacey was not so convinced but moments later she realised she was being observed through a quizzing glass. She stiffened under the scrutiny and after hesitating slightly the lady came forward.

"Miss Trevallion, is it not?"

"Indeed, ma'am."

Lady Moncourt eyed the woman with amusement.

"Miss Trevallion, allow me to present Lady Whitmore."

Obligingly Jacey curtsied and the woman smiled. "You are quite charming, as I have already observed. It is a mercy that you favour your dear Mama."

Jacey's eyes opened wide. "Did you know my Mama?"

Lady Whitmore smiled. "She was my kinswoman, a cousin. I was used to be very fond of her before her marriage." She glanced at Lady Moncourt curiously before returning her attention to Jacey. "Your betrothal has taken us all aback somewhat, but there is no doubt you have done well for yourself. Felicitations are in order."

"You are most kind, Lady Whitmore."

The woman smiled again. "Not at all. The family rift always seemed so foolish to me and no one regretted it more than I." She paused for a moment before adding, "No doubt we shall meet again before long."

So saying she swept away and Jacey said, gasping slightly, "She is the first of my mother's relatives I have ever encountered."

Lady Moncourt's lips curved into a wry smile. "You are certain to encounter more from now onwards. When you are Lady Sheringham your invitations will be eagerly sought and no one will wish to be excluded."

This aspect of her forthcoming marriage had not occurred to Jacey before. It was her first intimation of the kind of power she would wield and the notion pleased her.

"That is indeed a misfortune for the Daytons. As

none of Mama's relatives have cared a jot for us in more than twenty years, I do not think I shall trouble to include them in any of my diversions."

Lady Moncourt laughed. "So you see, there are compensations."

As she cast her an amused look, Jacey answered, "I only hope that they are great enough. Lady Moncourt, you will help me, won't you? I shan't know how to begin."

"You may, of course, always rely upon me. However, I am persuaded you will contrive very well. The one thing I will teach you is the cut. It will be most useful, I fancy, for setting down those you dislike."

They walked out into the wintry sunshine once more and Jacey's mood of despondency had given way to one of enjoyment. Lady Moncourt escorted her to several more shops where she was received in a toadying fashion by the owners. Jacey herself received the warmest welcome when it was discovered that she was to be the Countess of Sheringham. She was human enough to enjoy it hugely and realised that, as Lady Moncourt had intimated, there were compensations to a loveless marriage.

"I declare it has been the most satisfying morning I have spent in a long time!" Lady Moncourt exclaimed when they departed from the last of the shops, having purchased a huge amount of goods.

"I do not know how I may thank you, my lady," Jacey said shyly.

The marchioness cast her a fond look. "Being included in the guest list for all your brilliant diversions at Sheringham House is all the thanks I shall ever require."

"Lady Moncourt, you shall always be the guest of honour!"

The marchioness continued to gaze at her for a moment before saying, "How I wish I had a daughter like you."

Jacey looked away in confusion, for she could hardly confess that she wished for nothing better than to have her as a mother, and not merely to set her free of Lord Sheringham either.

A passing phaeton came to a standstill in the middle of the road, holding up all other traffic in a heedless manner. Jacey suddenly became aware of a stirring of excitement all around. When she looked up it was to see a stout young man in the driving seat, accompanied by a rather plain but pleasant-looking woman of a similar age to Lady Moncourt.

The marchioness was curtseying low as she said, "Your Royal Highness! What an unlooked for pleasure and an honour this is."

"Lady Moncourt, I admire your team. They are a fine pair of cattle. I have rarely seen such fine horses."

"Why, thank you, Sir. Such praise from so expert an eye is commendation enough."

"Should you ever wish to sell, pray let me be the first to know."

"It would be an honour, Sir." She glanced at Jacey who was staring unashamedly at the Prince of Wales. "Allow me to present to you the future Countess of Sheringham."

It was Jacey's turn to curtsey deeply as the Prince eyed her through his quizzing glass. "A fetching chit, I own. Sheringham has done well, but no doubt she will, like all females, improve with the years. What do you say, Lady Moncourt?"

"I am in agreement with you, Sir."

"Good day to you, madam," he said, waving his whip in the air.

The phaeton moved off and Jacey cried, "I can scarce believe he has noticed me!"

Lady Moncourt stared after the phaeton, smiling wryly. "If you were ten years older and a little rounder in build, you would be subjected to a great deal more of his attention than you would like. When I am at Carlton House, I am for ever evading his embrace."

Jacey laughed. "I wouldn't dare."

The marchioness cast her a mocking look. "If you can resist Sheringham's charm ..."

When they had climbed up on to the seat, Jacey asked, "Who was the woman accompanying him?"

"That was Maria Fitzherbert."

"Mrs. Fitzherbert! Poor Princess Caroline. How badly he treats her. I should not be able to bear it."

"Prinny is not the best of husbands – to either of his wives – I fear."

"Mrs. Fitzherbert looks to be sweet-natured, but she is not as beautiful as I had supposed."

"Who knows what it takes to capture the heart of a man? I wish I did."

For a moment she looked downcast, but then she urged on her team and the phaeton moved off.

"How well you handle the team," Jacey told her. "You drive as well as any man."

"Thank you, my dear. That is praise indeed. Would you care to take the riboons for a while?"

The offer caused Jacey to draw back in surprise. "I should be afraid to, my lady."

"I did not suppose to hear such words from the lips of Johnnie Trevallion's daughter."

Jacey smiled faintly. "At Trevallion Manor I often drove a gig around the estate and along our local roads, but there was little fear of meeting other vehicles, apart from the occasional farm cart, and if I did I was always given right of way. In Town everyone believes they are entitled to it."

"You would soon grow used to it. It is still early so mayhap you would like to practise for a while in the Park. It is too early for others to be there, only the demi-reps perhaps, and I dare say they will not deter you."

"Lady Moncourt, I hardly dare say yes. for you have already devoted so much time to me."

Ignoring her protests Lady Moncourt drove towards the Park. There was certainly less activity there than on Jacey's last visit with Sir John. A herd of grazing cows ignored the thunder of the wheels as Lady Moncourt drove past.

When she slowed down she handed the ribbons to Jacey, whose eyes glowed with anticipation as she took them. She drove at first slowly and then, as her confidence increased, with more dash, laughing out loud all the time.

"This is splendid!"

"You are doing very well," Lady Moncourt told her, raising her voice in order to be heard.

"It is good of you to say so, but I have yet to brave the streets of London. That will be the real test."

"You have negotiated all the other riders most prettily. You will soon be ready to take to the road."

Jacey laughed. "Aunt Minerva would have the vapours if she could see me!"

The carriage jerked over hillocks and into pot holes, but Jacey felt only exhiliration at gaining a new skill, and Lady Moncourt did not complain.

Suddenly, though, ahead of them a group of riders came galloping towards the phaeton. Jacey slowed the carriage to a more sedate pace only to realise that accompanying the group of several lovely ladies and elegant gentlemen was none other than the Earl of Sheringham.

For a moment the unexpectedness of seeing him and in the company of ladies of doubtful character, stunned her. She was at a loss what to do. He was obviously as surprised as she.

When she caught sight of them, too, Lady Moncourt said, "Oh dear, mayhap I should not have brought you here. What a chuckle-head, I am."

"We have as much right to be here as anyone, Lady Moncourt," Jacey declared, and as the group passed and the gentlemen raised their hats, she urged on the team once more and the carriage tore past the riders, jerking and bouncing over the path.

It was in Jacey's mind to put as great a distance between them as was possible, and once that was achieved she tried to slow the team down again. Her gentle effort had no effect and she pulled harder on the reins.

Only a few moment's later she realised to her horror that the horses, delighted at being given their head by so inexperienced a driver were totally out of control.

Jacey cried out in alarm as the phaeton thundered on, apparently gaining speed as it rattled on downhill. Lady Moncourt and her servant could only hold on desperately.

"What shall I do?" Jacey cried.

"Rein in!" the marchioness answered, shouting to be heard.

"I have done. It's no use! They don't respond!"

The Serpentine was ahead of them, gleaming in the sunlight.

"Oh, my goodness!" Jacey cried as it came nearer at an alarming speed.

Suddenly a rider drew alongside. Jacey, still clinging on to the reins, was scarcely aware of him, moving ahead, and then incredibly jumping from his own horse on to one of those attached to the phaeton.

For a few moments, as he struggled to bring the team under control, it seemed he would not succeed, but just when it appeared the horses, carriage and occupants would plunge into the icy waters of the Serpentine the phaeton shuddered to a halt.

Jacey sat in her seat stunned with the shock of their close escape, but Lady Moncourt immediately cried, "Oh, well done, Sheringham!"

He jumped down then, taking a few seconds to calm the horses which were snorting and steaming after such exertion. Two of his friends rode up at that moment, voicing concern for them, but Jacey was hardly aware of them either.

"Phaetons are not meant for racing, ma'am, but you'll be glad to learn your team is unhurt."

"Splendid. I have plans for them and it would be devilishly awkward if they were damaged in any way."

He glanced at Jacey then. "Miss Trevallion, are you hurt?"

She managed to shake her head and then turned to the marchioness. "Lady Moncourt, I do beg your pardon. How reckless of me to put us all at risk."

Lady Moncourt shrugged eloquently as she straightened her hat. "It could have happened to any of us. We have all had runaway teams. Have we not,

Sheringham?"

"Yes, ma'am," he replied, but Jacey did not entirely believe him. He was far too good a horseman to suffer such a calamity.

"I trust that you are also unharmed, my lady."

She laughed a little breathlessly. "Indeed, thanks to your bravery."

"I shall be reckless to the last."

Lady Moncourt laughed. "If that is so you must purchase a gig for your bride. She enjoys tooling the ribbons."

"Yes, ma'am, I shall do so, but I may also engage a man to drive it for her," he added dryly.

Lady Moncourt climbed down, leaving Jacey still sitting in the phaeton. "How shabby of you to say so, Sheringham. I thought she did very well."

"May I drive you back home, my lady?" he enquired, still glancing worriedly at Jacey.

"My house is but a short distance from here. Mayhap, Sir Phillip would accompany me, and you, Lord Sheringham, take Miss Trevallion to Bedford Square. I fear she is more shaken than she will admit."

"My pleasure," Sir Phillip admitted as Jacey looked at her in horror, but she was already moving away and in conversation with the young man who immediately dismounted from his horse.

The earl climbed up in her place saying, "I shall return your phaeton to Park Lane in due course, my lady."

The marchioness turned to give him a gracious smile. "I should be obliged if you would do so and then be good enough to have the team delivered to the Prince of Wales at Carlton House. He has only just admired them."

Lord Sheringham laughed. "I will do so with pleasure, ma'am."

The phaeton jerked into motion and the marchioness cast Jacey a gay wave before turning to converse with Sir Phillip again. Jacey stole a fearful glance at the earl as the marchioness began to walk away.

"You must think me a chuckle-head."

"On the contrary, I have rarely seen a woman handle a team so well. One error can be discounted or at least excused."

She stared at him in astonishment as he added, "It is only to be hoped you did not make that error in the hope of avoiding me."

He glanced at her, smiling wryly. "But I cannot truly believe you would do so. There is scarce a reason. No one has yet called me an ogre, and I know you are too well bred for actual rudeness."

Jacey could only listen to him in silence but then she was forced to retort, "Would you also have me acknowledge your companions?"

"Sir Phillip and Mr. Blackstock?"

Irritated she snapped, "The females."

"I am not acquainted with them. They were following us, no doubt, as is their custom, but they were not with us. However, that is of no account to you, Miss Trevallion."

She cast him a hate-filled look and then to her surprise, as they came to the end of Oxford Street he slowed the phaeton and held out the ribbons to her.

Immediately she drew back, "I couldn't."

His eyes were filled with a familiar mockery once more. "I had not thought you so faint-hearted, Miss Trevallion."

Rising to his teasing she snatched at the ribbons and set the team into motion again. It was one thing to drive beneath Lady Moncourt's benevolent eye, but quite another to be subjected to his critical scrutiny.

He sat back, apparently enjoying the ride, and Jacey was more than a little relieved when they arrived back at Bedford Square with no further mishap a very short time later.

"Well done," he told her as he handed her down.

Her cheeks flushed with colour as she replied, "Thank you, my lord."

"We have an engagement for dinner in the near future," he ventured and she nodded. "My mother is most anxious to make your acquaintance."

Jacey's heart filled with dread as he added, with no attempt to hide his irony, "No doubt you are equally as anxious to be acquainted with her."

She could only smile faintly and nod her head.

He raised his hat. "I must take my leave of you for now."

"Of course," she answered breathlessly. "I am obliged to you for your assistance."

"You need not speak of it. I could scarce allow you to go to the altar in a Bath Chair."

She could not help but chuckle at the notion. "The water looked exceeding cold."

"I have no doubt that it is."

He walked back to the phaeton, leaving her to feel unusually confused. It seemed, in his own strange way, he had tried to be pleasant to her.

When he reached the phaeton he turned to where she still stood outside the house. "This has been a very odd day. Now, I am obliged to turn lackey and deliver a team of horses to the Prince of Wales."

When he drove away, waving to her as he did so, she began to chuckle again and was still laughing when she finally went inside the house.

Eleven

Jacey's eyes opened wide when she first saw her aunt, gowned and ready to depart for Sheringham house. As Jacey drew on her own gloves she gazed in amazement at the figure Aunt Minerva presented in magenta silk, a jewelled turban on her head.

"Aunt Minerva, your gown is magnificent! Why have I not seen it before?"

"Because it is new, dear."

Jacey continued to look bewildered and her aunt explained, "Trevallion insisted upon it."

"But you know the state of his finances; they are severly strained, Aunt."

"Indeed, no one is more aware of it than I, and I would have refused his generosity only it suddenly occured to me that if I did not allow him to spend the blunt he was like to game it away in any event."

Jacey smiled then. "How right you are and you do look all the crack."

"Thank you, dear. Trevallion was determined I should not present a shabby figure at Sheringham House tonight. Even if we are in dun territory there is no need to shout it to the world."

"You will certainly put me to shame."

Miss Trevallion laughed. "Hardly, my dear, for it is

you who has youth and beauty, and there is no doubt you will be of the greatest interest to all who are present tonight."

"Oh, do not remind me of it! I am in a fidge at the very thought."

"I dare say you will find Lady Sheringham as amiable as her son."

Jacey laughed at that notion, although it was true she had harboured less virulent thoughts about him since his spirited rescue of her.

Miss Trevallion glanced worriedly at the grandfather clock in the corner. "I do hope your Papa is not going to be as usual late this evening. I did press upon him the importance of his being punctual on this occasion."

"You expect the impossible, Aunt Minerva. I suspect Papa was born late."

"How right you are! He was indeed, and has followed suit in everything he has done ever since."

She cast her niece a critical look. "I am so glad to see some colour in your cheeks, me dear. You have been so pale of late."

"My cheeks are flushed only because I fear the evening. I am persuaded I shall make a cake of myself in front of Lady Sheringham."

"That is a great improvement, too, for you was never used to care."

"For Papa's sake I must gain her approval, Aunt. It would be too awful if she prevailed upon Sheringham to cry off."

"I doubt if she will be able to do that. Your connections are good, if not your fortune, although that obviously suffices."

The door opened and Miss Trevallion turned on her heel. "Ah, Trevallion, here at last. We were in quite a fidge lest you be late."

"I wouldn't dare," he answered, his eyes wide. "Between you, Lady Moncourt and Fanny Sheringham, a fellow could be frightened out of his wits." He looked from one to the other. "I declare Lady Sheringham will find no fault with your appearance, my dears."

They went out into the hall where the house-steward and footman helped them into their outdoor attire.

As they went out to the waiting carriage Sir John looked at his daughter intently before saying, "I really think you are far too superior for Sheringham after all. I wish now I had cast the dice with the Duke of Pendarrass."

Jacey cast him an outraged look. "I doubt if anyone else would have been patient enough to await settlement of a debt, and not many men would agree payment of this kind. It is as well you shook dice with Sheringham after all."

Sir John was taken aback by her strictures. "My dear girl, that is the first time I have heard you take Sheringham's part," adding in hurt tones as he closed the carriage door behind him, "I am quite out of countenance."

* * *

Sheringham House was a handsome early Georgian mansion situated on the south side of Manchester Square. It was well-lighted so they had a good view of it as they approached.

To Jacey's alarm there were already several carriages outside.

"I do hope we are not late."

"My dear girl, what is late?" her father asked, adopting a fashionably languid air. "Whoever comes to time in this Town?"

"Some people do, Papa, as you can see."

They entered the handsome hall and several liveried servants came forward to divest them of their mantles.

"This is very handsome, Jacey," her aunt whispered glancing around with evident satisfaction. "I am happy that Sheringham will not oblige you to live shabbily."

"Would I consider such a match for my only daughter?" Sir John asked as he adjusted his neckcloth.

"I do hope you are not going to claim credit for this match," his sister scolded, "for little credit is due to *you.*"

"Heaven protect me from acid-tongued females," he complained.

"Oh, do stop quarrelling," Jacey begged as she glanced at her reflection in the mirror. "We are about to go up."

The house-steward led them up to the sitting room and all the while Jacey's heart beat unevenly. When the servant flung open the doors their arrival was announced and she took a deep breath before entering.

Fortunately the first person she saw was Lady Moncourt who was reclining on a sofa, swishing her fan to and fro. She cast an encouraging smile in Jacey's direction. When the girl dared to glance around her eyes immediately alighted upon the earl who came up to them.

"I do trust we are not late," she ventured.

"Not at all. Pray allow me."

He tucked her arm into his whilst Sir John accepted a glass of wine from a proferred tray and Miss Trevallion went to join an acquaintance.

The earl led her across the room past several guests with whom she was well-enough acquainted to cast a faint smile in their direction. She walked across the vastness of the carpet towards a sofa where the Dowager Countess of Sheringham sat in solitary splendour.

Gowned in blue taffeta, with a collar of diamonds about her throat, she appeared to be as daunting as Jacey had supposed. She was peering at Jacey down her high-bridged nose and her lips seemed to be pinched into an expression of disapproval.

As Jacey came closer to her, Lady Sheringham lifted her quizzing glass and studied her with even more care. Jacey stiffened under the scrutiny and automatically her head came up proudly.

"You are not on your way to Tyburn, you know," whispered the earl, which caused her to stiffen further.

"From all I have heard it would be a kinder fate."

He laughed softly before asking, "Have you recovered your mishap of the other day?"

The reminder amused her and she relaxed immediately, answering, "Yes, I thank you. I trust you delivered the team safely to the Prince."

"He is childishly pleased with his gift although I dare say he knew Lady Moncourt would give them to him when he praised their worth."

"What will she do without her horses?"

"Oh, she has already purchased a better pair. I am all admiration. Mama, allow me to present Miss Jacey Trevallion."

Lady Sheringham allowed her quizzing glass to drop as Jacey sank into a deep curtsey, mainly because it precluded the need to look upon that proud countenance which cast her into so much fear.

The dowager reached out with a heavily bejewelled hand and directed Jacey to sit at her side on the sofa.

"Sheringham, you may leave us now to have a coze."

"Certainly, Mama."

As he turned away, Jacey watched him go, feeling even more dismayed. There were a good many people in the room, all conversing easily. For the first time in her life, however, Jacey was at a loss for words.

"So you are to be my son's bride," the dowager began, and Jacey smiled at her hopefully. "I confess," the woman went on, "that when my son informed me he was to marry I was not only surprised at the suddeness of the decision, but also curious as to whom he deemed fit to become Countess of Sheringham."

Jacey's heart sank and whilst she was desperately trying to think of something to say in reply the dowager continued, "He speaks well of you which is natural, but you have, I understand, spent much of your life in the country. You must know that my son is not a rustic. You will find he prefers living in Town for most of the year, when he is not running off to Brighton with the Prince. As to that, my dear, you must use your womanly wiles to extract him from the rackety ways of the Carlton House Set. I do not altogether approve of their dissipated ways, although I am the first to admit we females do not hold a great deal of sway with our menfolk. It is enough we respect our duty to our husbands and family. The Sheringham title is an old one and you must, of course, make certain it continues."

Jacey was beginning to feel distinctly uncomfortable and her head swam. She glanced around to see Sir John in conversation with Lady Moncourt and Sheringham was casting worried glances in her direction from time to time. As well he might, she thought vexedly. No doubt he knew his mother very well indeed.

Lady Sheringham rapped her sharply on the knuckles with her fan, making Jacey start. "You do not appear to have much to say, Miss Trevallion."

"Begging your pardon ma'am, but you have given me little opportunity as yet."

The moment she had spoken Jacey bit her lip apprehensively, but it seemed that Lady Sheringham did not take her words amiss.

"Then we must certainly set aside a time so that you may. You certainly do not favour your Mama in that, nor, I fancy, Sir John."

"Did you know Mama?"

The dowager sniffed derisively. "We were acquainted. I know her family tolerably well."

"They never wished to know us."

Lady Sheringham allowed herself a thin-lipped smile. "I don't doubt they will wish to do so now."

"So I am told. Mama and Papa eloped, you see. It was frowned upon by Lord Dayton, my grandfather."

"I do recall the occasion. It was very foolhardy. Such behaviour does not augur well for the future."

"They were in love."

"Love is all very well for the lower orders, Miss

Trevallion, but what of duty?''

Jacey bit her lip in distress once more and tears came to her eyes.

"I do not approve of runaway marriages," the dowager went on. "They invariably come to grief, I find."

"My parents' marriage was exceeding happy."

"An isolated occurrence. Nothing will persuade me to the contrary. There is a romantic connotation to runaway marriages which I could never see for myself."

To Jacey's utter relief the lackey announced dinner and Sir John came striding across the room towards them.

"May I have the honour of taking you into dinner, my lady?"

The dowager got to her feet and her severe features softened into a smile which immediately made her look years younger, and far less daunting. Unfortunately it had taken Sir John to elicit it from her.

"Indeed you may, Sir John."

Out of the corner of her eye Jacey saw Lord Sheringham approaching her, but before he was halfway across the room a familiar voice asked, "Accord me the honour of taking you in to dinner, Miss Trevallion."

She looked up to see Geoffrey Pringle gazing at her. She got quickly to her feet, her eyes opening wide with surprise. This was the pleasantest happening in a thoroughly unpleasant evening.

"Mr. Pringle, I did not look to see you here tonight."

His handsome face broke into a crooked grin. "I am

family, Miss Trevallion."

She looked even more pleased. "That is indeed welcome news. I had no notion."

The young man looked abashed. "I am connected to the poor end of the family, needless to say, but Lady Sheringham has a strong sense of duty."

Jacey made a wry face. "So she has told me, in no uncertain terms!"

They began to walk towards the dining room and he said, "I hope you have received all my flowers, Miss Trevallion."

Her cheeks coloured. "And the marchpane. You are recklessly generous."

"If only I had the means to be more generous, Miss Trevallion. I am aware my regard is not enough."

To reach the dining room she was obliged to pass Lord Sheringham. Fearfully she raised her eyes to meet his and almost recoiled from the fury evident upon his face. She supposed he had assumed he had been snubbed. She had not intended it to be so, merely she was anxious not to have to speak with him just yet. For some reason it seemed important to avoid him and the presence of Geoffrey Pringle ensured that she would.

Twelve

Lady Sheringham sat at the head of the table, her son
at one hand and Jacey on the other. As the dishes were
passed around Lady Moncourt leaned across the table
and whispered:

"How did you fare?"

"Atrociously. I made quite a cake of myself."

"I'm certain you are mistaken, my dear, for if it was
so Lady Sheringham would have made her
disapproval known by now."

"I thought that she had."

As the meal progressed she tried to attend to Mr.
Pringle's bright conversation but found it difficult, for
Lord Sheringham often fixed her with a dark,
brooding gaze which was disturbing. No doubt he was
wondering about her conversation with his mother,
but he would learn the dowager's version of it from her
own lips all too soon.

As she gazed around the table everyone seemed in
high spirits which irked in view of her own discomfort.
Aunt Minerva was seated next to a stout gentleman
who attended her every word with the gravity she
would appreciate, and Lady Moncourt's eyes gleamed
as Sir John explained some matter to her at great
length.

Poor Lady Moncourt, Jacey found herself thinking;
for all her wealth and beauty she is as wretched as I.

"You do not eat a great deal, Miss Trevallion."

At the sound of the dowager's voice Jacey returned
her attention and smiled wanly. "I cannot think why,
ma'am. The food is quite exceptional."

"My cook is the finest," she agred with no attempt
at modesty.

"If Miss Trevallion does not eat it is, mayhap,
because you have frightened her out of her wits,
Mama," the earl supplied, much to Jacey's chagrin.

His perception was quite alarming. She only hoped
it was not always so accurate.

"I?" the dowager asked, laughing in bewilderment.
"I cannot believe that is true. Do I alarm you, Miss
Trevallion?"

"Lord Sheringham is gammoning you," Jacey
managed to answer, feeling acutely uncomfortable.

"He is such a funster," his mother replied, raising
her quizzing glass at Mr. Pringle who, unlike Jacey,
ate with gusto. "Now, Geoffrey, how does your mother
do?"

"She is in rude health, I thank you, ma'am, and
sends her felicitations."

"I am delighted to hear it. How do you do of late,
my boy?"

"Tolerably well, ma'am. I do however often find life
... frustrating."

He glanced at Jacey who coloured slightly and the
dowager laughed. "It is for us all, my boy. Tell me, do
you still intend to join the army?"

"It is still my intention to do so when I am able,
ma'am, but when that may be I cannot be sure."

"The ambition is admirable enough. With more

fighting men of Decourcy character in the army we should have won this wretched war against the French years ago.''

"I am a Pringle, ma'am,'' he reminded her.

Lady Sheringham looked vexed. "Your mama is a Decourcy. That is all which matters.''

"With that in view, ma'am, I declare we should have won if you were one of His Majesty's generals.''

Jacey was hard put not to laugh, but she stifled it for she was certain Mr. Pringle was being facetious. However, Lady Sheringham found the notion amusing.

"You are no doubt correct. I would certainly know what advice to give Wellesley. He obviously does not have suitable advisors.''

From across the table the earl caught Jacey's eye. He, too, appeared amused but she quickly averted her eyes rather than return his smile. The problem was that she felt so confused. Lady Sheringham's haughty attitude was a mere irritant. Jacey was more concerned for her own attitude towards the earl. He was such a puzzle to her, sometimes attentive and occasionally aloof.

"I had no notion you were about to enlist, Mr. Pringle,'' she said a few moments later when Lady Sheringham's attention was engaged elsewhere.

"As a younger son of an already impoverished family, some occupation is very necessary. It is my misfortune being obliged to apply to Sheringham for the means to purchase my commission.''

He reached for a bunch of grapes which rested on the epergne on the centre of the table.

Jacey gave him a sympathetic look. "How well I know the ignominy of being indebted to another.''

"You need say no more. 'Tis enough I am devastated. I have never had cause to envy my cousin his elevated situation or his wealth, but I do envy him his bride. I do pray that you will forgive me my impudence in saying so."

"On the contrary I am warmed by your regard," she answered, but her heart felt unaccountably heavy.

Her cheeks had coloured at his fulsome praise and at that moment her eyes met those of the earl's. His face remained inscrutible but she had the oddest feeling he knew the gist of the conversation, something which caused her colour to deepen even more.

It was a relief when the ladies ajourned to the drawing room to take coffee during which time Lady Sheringham gave forth on various topics and all others present listened raptly.

At one point Lady Moncourt gave her a knowing smile and Jacey responded but with less certainty. When the men eventually joined them they were considerably merrier, no doubt due to the port they had consumed in the meantime.

Mr. Pringle, much to her pleasure and embarrassment, gravitated to her side with very little delay. His partiality was most marked and becoming more so every time they met. In other circumstances Jacey would have been delighted. She found him an amiable companion and her portion would have made her an ideal partner for him. However, in view of her coming marriage Jacey dare not allow herself to become too attached. Such behaviour would be foolhardy, but it was difficult not to enjoy his undemanding company.

"Mayhap Miss Trevallion will entertain us on the harpsichord," Lady Sheringham suggested, fixing

Jacey with a look which plainly dared her not to be able.

For a moment Jacey was stunned and could neither move nor reply, but then Sir John came to her rescue by saying in a characteristically hearty way, "Your choice is admirable, my lady. My daughter is exceeding accomplished."

"Let us hear for ourselves, Sir John. I do not think you are in a fair position to judge."

Most welcomingly Mr. Pringle was at her side. "Allow me, Miss Trevallion."

She cast him a grateful smile and allowed him to escort her across the room to the instrument, aware that all eyes were upon her, especially those of Lady Sheringham. When they reached the harpsichord the earl was already there, which caused her to hesitate somewhat before she sat down.

Sheringham cast his cousin a cold look before saying, "I thank you, Pringle, but I shall remain to turn Miss Trevallion's music. Charming as she is, you cannot be allowed to monopolise her all evening."

Geoffrey Pringle hesitated, too, looking more than a little vexed at his cousin's sarcastic manner, but he had no choice but to withdraw. Jacey felt it would be altogether too much to play under the earl's close scrutiny as well as that of his mother. However, with trembling hands she chose a piece of music which was mercifully familiar and began to play.

At first she was hesitant, aware of the interest shown towards Sheringham's bride-to-be and the proximity of the earl himself, but then, realising she was not disgracing herself after all, gained confidence. She glanced at him to note his expression was bland. If only, she thought, I could have an inkling of what he was really thinking. Good breeding and manners were sometimes a hopeless bar to true feelings.

The room was unusually quiet and it seemed all the guests were determined to judge her accomplishments. Some of her old spirit came to the fore and, casting a glance at Lady Sheringham, who was toying with her fan, Jacey began to sing the words to the tune, too.

It was not until she had played and sung the last note that she regretted being so rash. She suspected that the talent which entertained her aunt in Cornwall did not sound quite so accomplished in the drawing rooms of the *ton*.

There was, however, a good deal of warm applause. As she got to her feet, relieved to be finished, foremost in the applause was her father and Lady Moncourt, and her heart warmed to them.

Lady Sheringham scarce put her hands together and as the applause died away Jacey heard the dowager say, "As a girl I had a delightful voice. I was always used to be prevailed upon to sing wherever I went."

This, Jacey took to be a tacit criticism of her own performance and her cheeks grew red.

"You are more accomplished then I dared to hope."

It was the earl's voice in her ear which made her turn to him sharply and retort, "But not nearly as accomplished as Lady Sheringham in her youth."

Wryly he smiled. "I am persuaded no one could be. Come, I have someone who wishes to met you."

Rather unwillingly she followed him across the room to where a dark-haired young woman who was rather stout but had pleasant features, was sitting on a sofa looking at her expectantly as she approached.

"Miss Trevallion, allow me to present my sister, Lady Wycherley."

Jacey was quite taken aback, for the woman looked nothing like the earl or his autocratic mother. Her smile, however, was most welcoming.

"Do sit down, my dear. I have been in a fidge all evening to have a coze with you."

Jacey sat down and noticed that the earl wandered away to seat himself next to a young woman who had been endeavouring to catch his attention all evening. For the first time she considered he might well be attractive to women. They all certainly fawned upon him, much as they did with Sir John.

"You cannot imagine how amazed we all were," Lady Wycherley was saying, "when Sheringham declared his intention of being wed, but it is not before it is due."

She chuckled and Jacey returned her attention to Lady Wycherley again. "You are very kind, ma'am."

"I insist that you call me Eliza. We shall be the greatest of friends; I know it."

Jacey began to warm to her future sister-in-law who was a pleasant surprise after the dowager. "I do hope so, ma'am." She blushed. "Eliza."

"You are just the bride I had always hoped my brother would choose." She chuckled again. "But in all honesty I feared he would never have the good sense to choose someone like you."

Jacey looked at her with interest. "I cannot conceive why. Sheringham is very eligible."

"Oh, he was always such a scapegrace. Mama and I feared that when he did decide to wed he might choose an altogether frightful creature. How odd it should be someone who is not even come out." She dimpled.

"But that is quite clever of him not to chance your being won by another. How did you meet?"

For a moment Jacey was at a loss how to answer and then she said quite truthfully, "It was through my father, Sir John Trevallion."

"Ah, yes. We are acquainted." She smiled. "Sir John I find vastly amusing. He is always in such spirits and full of charm. No one can possibly be downcast for long in his company. Even Mama likes him, and she would find fault with a fat goose."

"I fear she will find me sadly lacking."

"That cannot be, I assure you. You must not mind Mama. I know that her manner is a trifle top-lofty, but I am persuaded she must be delighted with you. How else can it be, my dear?"

Jacey was grateful for her praise, but she was not so easily convinced and her head was beginning to ache abominably. The evening had been a sore trial and even now seemed endless.

"When you have returned from your wedding trip you must call upon me in Brook Street."

"It would be my honour, Eliza."

"I cannot wait for you to visit my nursery. We have three children, two girls and a boy. Quinn dotes upon them."

Jacey frowned. "Quinn?"

It was Lady Wycherley's turn to look taken aback. "My brother Sheringham."

"Eliza! Eliza, my dear," Lady Sheringham called. "Do be pleased to play for us on the harp before supper is served. You play so well, your accomplishment is an example for us all."

Eliza turned to Jacey and sighed. "I am afraid Mama will not be gainsaid." She patted Jacey's hand.

"We will talk again, and at more length on the next occasion."

Jacey smiled warmly. "Indeed. It will be a pleasure and I look forward to it."

Lady Wycherley went across the room and towards the harp. Jacey's head was thumping louder than ever and the buzz of conversation all around did not help to alleviate it.

As Lady Wycherley seated herself at the harp there was a sudden lull in the conversation, during which Lady Sheringham could be heard to say, "I do so agree, my dear. So many scions of great houses are marrying beneath themselves these days. Duty speaks for nothing with them, I fear."

The comment caused fury to well upon within Jacey's breast. She had no doubt that the barb was meant for her and yet there was nothing she could say to counter it. She was terrified lest Lady Sheringham discover the true reason for the marriage.

Just then she was assailed with the desire to flee the house, even the city, and run as far as she could to escape this intolerable situation. How long ago it seemed since she had left Trevallion Manor, full of excitement and expectation. Just then she was furious with her father for putting her in such an invidious position, but at that moment he smiled across at her and the feeling died.

As Lady Wycherley began to pluck at the strings of the harp, Jacey got up and slipped out into the hall, putting two hands to her aching head. To her surprise her eyes were filled with tears, too.

She sank back against the panelling, enjoying the coolness through her gown. The thought of marriage to Lord Sheringham was a dreadful one, and yet if he were to cry off, the result would mean disaster for Sir John, and she knew she could not bear that.

A footstep in the doorway made her stiffen with alarm, but she relaxed a little more when she saw that it was merely Mr. Pringle.

"Miss Trevallion, I saw you leave the drawing room. I trust you are not indisposed."

"'Tis merely a headache, Mr. Pringle. Nothing to be concerned about, but I do thank you for your concern."

He came towards her looking worried. "On the contrary, I believe your carriage should be called."

Her eyes grew wide. "Oh, no. I cannot leave so early in the evening. Lady Sheringham will think me a poor creature."

He smiled then. "She cannot possibly be so foolish."

"You are far too kind to me, Mr. Pringle."

"Would it were possible for me to lavish my true feelings upon you," he said in heartfelt tones, looking at her longingly. "There is so much I would wish to say to you, Miss Trevallion."

"You must not," she gasped, feeling suddenly trapped.

To stay would be foolhardy, and yet to return to the drawing room meant facing the earl and his mother.

All at once she was afraid, although of what she could not be certain. It was definite that Geoffrey Pringle posed no threat to her.

She began to move toward the drawing room once again. "I must return to the others. It would not do if we were missed."

As she made to go past him she swayed slightly. He

caught her hand, looking even more concerned than before.

"Have a care, Miss Trevallion. Mayhap, I should call Miss Minerva, for I am of the opinion you really should return home."

She shook her head stubbornly. "I am quite all right, I thank you."

When she looked up at him it was to wonder how it would feel to be kissed by him. The memory of the earl's kiss had been one she had fought to forget. That was proving impossible.

"Miss Trevallion," he whispered, moving even closer. "Jacey ..."

As if in a dream she moved nearer to him. His arm was about her waist, his face very close to hers. She had to know what it was like to be kissed by another man.

"I hope I do not intrude."

She jumped back in alarm. Mr. Pringle grew pale at the sight of his cousin in the doorway of the drawing room, looking for all the world as if he might kill the pair of them.

"Lady Sheringham wishes to speak with you, Pringle," he said, never taking his eyes from Jacey's stricken face.

If she had experienced wretchedness before it was nothing to what she felt at that moment, for she could readily envisage the picture the pair of them had made just about to kiss.

Geoffrey Pringle cast her one last, longing look before he went back into the drawing room. Jacey began to follow, hating the thought of being forced to pass so close to the earl.

It seemed, however, he had no intention of allowing her to pass. He stood four-square in the doorway, eyeing her coldly. It was the most daunting experience of her life, being the recipient of his wrath.

"So, you are not averse to the embrace of all men."

"You are mistaken, my lord, in what you believed you witnessed."

"Please spare me the Banbury Tale. There is nothing wrong with my eyesight."

She looked up at him then, her eyes blazing, caution gone. "Very well. If you wish to make more of it, you did indeed see Mr. Pringle embrace me. How shocking! But no more shocking than when it was you, I assure you!"

There was no change in his demeanour as he answered, "The difference is that you are the future Countess of Sheringham, and he is well aware of it."

"Men are such hypocrites!"

"Moreover, I believe his attachment to you is merely to provide an irritant to me."

Jacey stamped her foot in fury. "No doubt he will beg your pardon most heartily for he, too, depends upon your charity for his well-being."

"He does not sing small my cousin, 'tis evident."

"He is wretched and with good reason. I wonder how many other poor wretches are indebted to you and are made to know it unendingly!"

His eyes flashed with fire, "Do you think so? Well, let me tell you about my cousin Pringle."

She made to go past him yet again. "I do not wish to know."

He caught her wrist in a vice-like grip, causing her to gasp. "Nevertheless, you will listen as intently as you listened to him." Her eyes blazed with defiance as he went on, "Pringle is as lazy as Ludlum and no victim of my oppression, as he has so obviously led you to believe. He left Cambridge only a year after he went up, under a cloud due to some matter concerning a young lady. During a Grand Tour of Europe he was thrown into a Neapolitan jail, from which I was obliged to extract him, and if I am less than eager to purchase a commission for him it is only because I value the good name of my mother's family and that of His Majesty's army."

Jacey was stung to think that so bland a young man could have been the perpetrator of so many wrongs and although she had no wish to hear of them from Sheringham's lips, she did not doubt for one moment that he spoke the truth.

"I think, Lord Sheringham," she answered breathlessly, "that you expect perfection in all those around you, and yet you do not practise it yourself. Moreover, you have a thought only for the rights of a matter and not the consequence."

His grip was no less tight as he said in a tone which alarmed her with its menace. "You should heed the consequence of your own actions, Miss Trevallion. I am growing heartily tired of your missish ways and you may be assured I shall not tolerate them indefinitely."

"What do you mean?"

He let her go and she rubbed her reddened wrist. "You will certainly discover my meaning before long."

"Miss Trevallion. *Miss Trevallion*! What are you doing lurking in the doorway? Sheringham, what can you be thinking of? Miss Trevallion is certain to catch a chill if she remains in the doorway. Bring her to me.

I wish to speak with her again."

Lady Sheringham's insistent voice shook Jacey, but no more than the menace in his tone. Trembling visibly she returned to the drawing room, followed by the earl at whom she dare not look for the remainder of the evening, although the menace in his voice repeatedly returned to haunt her.

Thirteen

Miss Trevallion laughed as she stepped into the hall and pulled off her bonnet. "La! I declare I have not enjoyed an outing more. The animals in the zoo were quite alarming, but of the greatest interest."

Following her aunt into the hall, Jacey felt less diverted by their outing. Several days had passed since the disastrous dinner at Lady Sheringham's, and since that night she had seen nothing of the earl, although his sister had called and seemed as amiable as before.

As Miss Trevallion looked through those cards which had been left in their absence she sighed, "I wonder where Sheringham can be? We have not set eyes on him for an age. Mayhap he has gone to the country." She brightened. "No doubt he has gone to give instructions for his house to be put in order for you, my dear."

Jacey did not answer. Her heart had been full of dread since her last fateful meeting with him. She knew now that if he cried off she would be devastated, and not only because of the effect upon her father.

"Did you know that Mr. Pringle has gone into the army?"

Jacey's eyes opened wide at this news. "No, I had no notion of it. This is sudden, is it not?"

"He was waiting for Sheringham to stump the blunt, which he has now done, according to Lady Moncourt. He is to leave for the fighting almost immediately." She eyed her niece warily. "I trust that this news does not grieve you, my dear. You seemed a mite attached to him."

"I cannot conceive what gave you such a notion," she answered breathlessly, averting her eyes.

"That is a great relief, as was the news of your escape from harm in Lady Moncourt's phaeton. When she told me of the incident I very nearly swooned."

Miss Trevallion put one hand to her breast and Jacey cried, "Oh, how shabby of her to tell you! I'd as lief you did not hear of it."

"I was gratified to hear it was Sheringham who came to your rescue. You were most fortunate he was to hand."

"He was," Jacey admitted heavily, "magnificent. He could have suffered grievous injury himself."

Miss Trevallion patted her hand. "I am persuaded you are now coming to appreciate his worth. Now I am going to rest before dinner. I am so pleased we have no engagements this evening; this life we lead of late has been wearing on my constitution."

Jacey smiled wanly as her aunt went up the stairs. When she had gone she took off her bonnet and looked in vain for some communication from Lord Sheringham.

"Is Sir John out?" she asked the house-steward as he came into the hall.

"Yes, ma'am. He went out yesterday evening and has yet to return."

Jacey stiffened. "Do you mean to say he has been out since last night?"

"Yes, ma'am."

"Some ill must have befallen him. Why did you not raise the alarm earlier?"

The house-steward smiled superciliously. "I beg your pardon, ma'am, but it is by no means uncommon for Sir John to stay out the entire night."

At this news Jacey's cheeks grew rather pink and to cover it she pulled herself to full height and said, "Will you kindly let me know the moment he returns?"

"Certainly, ma'am, but I feel it right to tell you Sir John has been known to stay away for several nights."

"Not when I am here!" she retorted, something which elicited a wry glance from the lackey.

As she turned away from him, feeling foolish as well as angry at her father, the front door opened and a missive was handed to one of the footmen.

"It is for you, ma'am," he informed her immediately.

Before he could bring it to her she ran forward and took it from him. Her heart began to beat fast as she wondered if this could be from Lord Sheringham at last. However, one glance at the unsealed scrap of paper told her it couldn't possibly be, and she didn't know whether to be glad or sorry.

Her finger's continued to tremble as she unfolded the paper. She couldn't imagine anyone she knew who would send such a disreputable-looking scrap. There were but a few words written on it in a scrawling hand she scarce recognised. As she read it her eyes filled with horror and she staggered backwards.

"No! Oh no! It cannot be! He wouldn't. He couldn't."

"Miss Trevallion?" asked the footman, looking concerned at her distress.

"'Tis nothing," she gasped, turning away, her mind filled with horror.

What shall I do? she thought in desperation, reading the note yet again.

Suddenly she snatched up her bonnet and rushed to the door, the note still crushed in her hand. Her thoughts were still frantic as she dashed out into the square. Fortunately a hackney carriage was passing by and she quickly waved him down. Giving Lady Moncourt's address to the driver she climbed inside, her thoughts still chaotic.

Throughout the journey to Park Lane Jacey sat in the smelly carriage, twisting her hands together in anguish.

"Oh, do hurry," she urged and jumped down as soon as she had reached Moncourt House. A second blow was to await her there, however.

"Lady Moncourt is not at home," her house-steward announced.

Tears of frustration came to Jacey's eyes then. "She must be due to return before long."

"I understand Lady Moncourt has gone out of Town today, madam, and I really cannot say when she will return. She has no engagement for this evening as far as I am aware."

Jacey bit her lip. She was very close to breaking down but contrived not to, as that would solve nothing. She knew it was important for her to remain calm.

"May I leave her ladyship a note?" she asked in no more than a whisper, not knowing what else to do. There was no one else who could help her now.

"Certainly, madam. Come this way."

He ushered her into a spacious library where there

was an ample supply of parchment, ink and wafers. Her writing was not of the neatest, for her hand shook all the while she was penning the note. Anger as well as despair tore at her heart as the pen stabbed at the parchment.

When she handed the note to the house-steward at last she said, "You will be sure to give this to Lady Moncourt as soon as she is returned. It is a matter of the utmost import."

"You may rely upon it, madam."

Outside the mansion Jacey almost gave way to her despair again and once more was obliged to fight her own emotions. No hackney carriages were to be seen so she hailed a sedan chair and wearily gave them the Bedford Square address. Her progress was altogether too slow but she acknowledged that there was nothing more she could do save await news of Lady Moncourt who was bound to know what action to take.

It was with a heavy heart that she paid the chairmen at the end of her journey. Now she had arrived home she was reluctant to go inside for fear of encountering her aunt who, on hearing the news, was bound to have an attack of the vapours – or worse.

Her head drooped as she turned towards the door, but then looked up hopefully at the approach of horses. Her entire demeanour froze at the sight of Lord Sheringham's curricle. Her heart filled with fury and hatred, tenfold anything she had experienced before.

As he climbed down, she cried, "Have you come to gloat?"

A look of puzzlement crossed his face. "Miss Trevallion?"

"I wonder that you dare to show your face here!

This is all your doing!" She waved the note in front of him. "You promised you would punish me, and now you have done so in the cruellest way. You have sent Papa to the Fleet! You are despicable!"

The tears could no longer be fought. Her voice broke as she lashed out at him with her fists. He deflected what was not, in any event, a hard blow and snatched the missive which she still clutched in one of her fists.

Glancing at it briefly he threw it to one side and climbed back into the curricle, driving away as if the Devil himself were in pursuit.

* * *

Still wearing her day gown Jacey sat at the edge of the sofa. Every so often the clock struck the quarter hour and her heart pounded with dread.

When the door clicked open at last she jumped to her feet and looked anxiously at the servant who had entered.

The footman bowed. "What time do you wish dinner to be served, ma'am?"

She looked away in despair. "I don't know. Later. It doesn't matter. Is there no word yet from Lady Moncourt?"

"No, ma'am."

"And Miss Trevallion? She is not yet down, is she?"

"No, ma'am."

That at least was a blessing. She dare not think the effect this would have upon her aunt, and Jacey was determined to keep the news from her for as long as was possible.

As the lackey bowed out of the room she became aware of a commotion in the hall and with no hesitation ran out of the drawing room past him. The front door was open and in came Sir John, looking less than his usual elegant self. His clothing was filthy and his hair was in disarray. Jacey had never in her life seen him look less than immaculate and the sight of him like this was in itself alarming.

"Papa!"

He smiled wanly, looking unusually fatigued. "Jacey, Jacey, my dear girl. What a mischance this has been."

With no further ado she launched herself into his arms, laughing and crying all at once. "Oh, Papa, what a fright you gave me. I nearly died of mortification when I read your note."

He patted her gently. "Now, now, my lovely, there's no need to get into a pucker over this. It is all finished now and we would do best to cast it from our minds."

As she searched his face anxiously for signs of a lie he held her away, saying, "I must get out of these clothes with no further delay. My God, what a place that is. I shouldn't have lasted a sen'night, I confess. It was good of Sheringham to fetch me out."

He glanced behind him and it was only then that Jacey saw the earl was there, too.

"Going to put some clean clothes on," Sir John announced, walking towards the stairs. "Stay a while, Sheringham. We'll break open a bottle of madeira." His face crinkled into a moue of distaste. "My God, these clothes smell foul."

Left alone with the earl, Jacey scarcely knew what to say. It was fortunate that he saved her the trouble.

He came towards her, removing his curly-brimmed beaver, but he made no attempt to take off his caped driving coat.

"Miss Trevallion, it may please you to know the person responsible for committing Sir John to the Fleet was a fellow by the name of Dalrymple, a shirt maker of St James' Street."

Tears trembled on her lashes as she looked up into his inscrutible face. "Lord Sheringham ..." she began, but her lips trembled too much to allow her to finish. Indeed she scarcely knew what she wished to say to him.

His eyes seemed to grow darker. "How could you think I would cause you such pain?"

"I don't know how ..." she began but he put on his hat and turned on his heel.

"Be pleased to give my excuses to Sir John, Miss Trevallion," and so saying he strode out of the house.

Jacey ran after him, but the curricle was already moving away at a fast pace.

"Oh, please!" she cried, but her words were lost on the wind.

Through blurred eyes she watched him out of sight, scarcely aware that another carriage had drawn up.

"Miss Trevallion!"

Jacey turned on her heel to see Lady Moncourt climbing down from her phaeton. She looked unusually ashen-faced.

"I have your note! I have been visiting an aunt at Knightsbridge and remained there all day. Come along; there is no time to lose. Let us go to the Fleet with all haste and fetch him away from that frightful place."

"Papa is already home, Lady Moncourt. All is

well," Jacey told her and her voice was husky with emotion. The marchioness looked taken aback and Jacey added, "Lord Sheringham has paid the debt and brought Papa home."

"Sheringham! But it was he ... Your note said he ..."

"I was mistaken. I put the saddle on the wrong horse."

She averted her eyes and after a moment's pause the marchioness said in a brisk manner, "Let us go inside. It would not do for you to catch a chill out here in the night air."

As they passed into the hall Sir John was coming down the stairs, having changed his filthy clothes for an outfit more like his usual style.

"Lady Moncourt!" he greeted her heartily, for all the world as if nothing were wrong.

"Trevallion, you coxcomb, I am as mad as a weaver at the fright you have given me and your poor daughter. We shall not forgive you lightly."

"You cannot hold me to blame for the impetuosity of a tradesman." He flicked open the lid of his snuffbox and took a pinch. "His shirts were somewhat inferior in any event."

"You are remarkable calm about it."

He cast her a devilish grin. "My dear Maria, it was evident to me I should not languish there for long."

"On this occasion, perhaps, but on another you might not be so fortunate."

He came down the stairs looking annoyed. "If you are set upon scolding me I shall not remain here to listen."

"What is all this about a fright?" Miss Trevallion asked, pausing on the landing to peer down at them.

"I'd as lief return to the Fleet as explain," Sir John murmured darkly, taking his hat, cane and cape from the house-steward.

With one backward glance at his sister he strode out of the house.

"Someone shall tell me," Miss Trevallion vowed as she came down the stairs. "What has my rackety brother been up to on this occasion?"

Lady Moncourt cast a worried look at Jacey who burst out at last, "It is all my doing, Aunt Minerva! I have been the most utter crack brain who ever lived!"

Her aunt looked astonished and more so as Jacey rushed past her up the stairs, sobbing heartbrokenly.

Calmly Lady Moncourt removed her gloves, saying, "I fear your niece is in love, my dear."

Miss Trevallion frowned. "In love with whom, pray tell me?"

"Lord Sheringham, of course!"

"Stuff and nonsense. Jacey has taken him in dislike. It is of the greatest concern to me, I assure you."

Lady Moncourt smiled as she handed the lackey her bonnet and pelisse. "Then you need be concerned no longer." She linked her arm into that of the bewildered Minerva Trevallion. "Come along to the drawing room, my dear, and let me explain ..."

Fourteen

Jacey stared at her face in the mirror before sighing and confiding in her maid, "I look quite hag-ridden. Is there nothing more you can do to make me look better?"

Rose brushed on a little more rouge and then began to pin up Jacey's curls. "It's not as bad as you suppose, ma'am, but some kind of reaction is only to be expected after such a to-do."

Jacey nodded. "I have experienced more emotion in this past few weeks than in the whole of my life before. Just to think, Rose, when I was at Trevallion Manor I wished so hard for something to happen. How I wish now I was back there and heartily bored!"

"You'll feel better once you're wed, ma'am," Rose told her soothingly, but that provided no balm for Jacey's heart.

She laughed harshly. "I don't even know if I am still to be wed, Rose. I have not set eyes upon Lord Sheringham in a sen'night. It was all I could do to stand still for the fitting of my gown the other day. It seemed such a waste of time."

"I don't suppose you have anything to fear, ma'am."

"No, indeed," Jacey murmured, sighing slightly.

"If Lord Sheringham wished to cry off, he would have done so by now."

"I am persuaded you are correct, Rose. There is no other way he can collect his debt; Papa will never be in sufficient funds to do so. However, I do take leave to doubt that there has ever been a wedding where the bride and groom are on such bad terms."

The maid chuckled. "From all I have heard, ma'am, it is usually so."

This statement did not comfort Jacey in the least, but she cast the girl a smile before she got to her feet.

She went downstairs slowly, feeling not the least like a prospective bride. A pile of cards were as usual awaiting her attention, but she had no mind to look at them, for she knew instinctively there would not be one from the earl. Several posies of flowers were awaiting her, too; she didn't even cast them a glance. Once she had disdained Sheringham's gifts, now she would have given anything for a token of regard from him.

"Sir John requests your presence in the drawing room, Miss Trevallion," the house-steward informed her.

Thinking it odd that her father should be at home at that time of the day, she went immediately to the drawing room, hoping fervently he was not in another difficult situation. Jacey was quite certain she could not withstand one more shock.

He was standing in front of the roaring fire, looking more than a little pleased with himself, something which caused Jacey to relax a little the moment she saw him. What did surprise her was the sight of Lady Moncourt who quickly moved away from Sir John as soon as the door opened.

On seeing her, Jacey immediately curtseyed. "Lady Moncourt, this is a great surprise. I did not look to see you here."

"A pleasant surprise, I trust."

For some reason the marchioness looked uncharacteristically uncomfortable.

"Oh, indeed."

The marchioness glanced at Sir John who said, after clearing his throat noisily, "Jacey, my dear, I have some good news to impart."

Cheered by the sight of Lady Moncourt, Jacey retorted, "That would be a delightful change. I have yet to hear any good news since my arrival in this Town."

Lady Moncourt frowned and Sir John peered at her worriedly. "You have been looking all done up these last few days. I do trust you are not about to fall foul of some ague."

She began to walk towards them. "You must not mind my megrims. I am being told at every turn that it is to be expected in a prospective bride."

Lady Moncourt looked none too convinced, but Jacey entreated, "Papa, do not delay imparting your good news. I am in a fidge to hear of it."

Sir John drew himself up to full height and Lady Moncourt sank down into a sofa, staring down at her gloved hands with undue interest.

"I have made an offer of marriage to Lady Moncourt, and she has honoured me by accepting."

Jacey's eyes grew round and then as her father watched her eagerly for her reaction, she cried, "That is splendid news, indeed!"

She didn't know to whom she should first go, but finally threw herself into Sir John's arms. "Oh, I shall not wish you happy for I know you will be!" She drew away from him then. "You are the most fortunate man alive, Papa."

"I know it, my lovely. To have the affection of two good women is far more than I deserve."

"Three, Papa. You must not forget Aunt Minerva's regard for you which is no less for not being overt."

"Then I am more fortunate than I know."

Then Jacey turned to the marchioness who reached out for her hand. "I am so pleased for you, my lady."

"Your Papa and I will deal famously together you may be sure."

"I am in no doubt of it, and I could not wish for better news."

Lady Moncourt reached to brush a tear from Jacey's cheeks. "My dear, I only hope that one day very soon you will be as happy as I am."

Jacey drew away, smiling uncertainly then. "You're very kind." She turned to her father. "Does Aunt Minerva know?"

"You are the very first," he assured her. "It is as we wished, for without your urging I doubt if I should ever have gained sufficient courage to come up to scratch."

"Then I beg of you both excuse me, for I would like to go and fetch her so you can impart the news to her."

"By all means," the marchioness told her happily.

Sir John walked with her to the door and when they reached it she said in a low voice, casting a glance back at Lady Moncourt, "Papa, what inspired you to come up to scratch? You were so set against it a few weeks ago."

"Only because of the dire state of my finances."

"Which has not changed."

"I have always been devilishly fond of the wench, as no doubt you've observed, and when I saw how concerned she was about my incarceration in the Fleet, I realised she did not care a jot about my lack of funds. Maria has no illusions about me – she cares for me just as I am – but I shall not disappoint her, Jacey. You may rely upon that."

"You will incur my wrath if you do!"

He looked suddenly serious. "You do realise what this means to you, do you not, my lovely?"

"Oh indeed, Papa; someone else, heaven be praised, will be responsible for worrying on your behalf."

He smiled. "I have been a sore trial to you, I know."

She put one hand on his. "I would not change you for a thousand worthy bores, Papa."

"You will not now be obliged to marry Sheringham." Her face stiffened. "I shall have the means to pay his debt, and all my others. I shall not be so foolish again. It almost breaks my spirit to realise what my rakehell ways almost did to you. At least I can make amends now. You're free to choose whom you will for a husband. There will be a score of them paying court to you once it is known you are free and I shall abide by your choice, be he a carpenter or a duke. The choice is entirely yours, you may be assured."

"Thank you, Papa," she murmured, looking away in distress.

"I had best get back to Maria. We have a multitude of arrangements to discuss. Be a dear and delay telling your aunt a little while longer."

"If that is your wish, Papa, but I cannot conceive why."

"Can you not?" he asked smiling roguishly. "When

she is given the news she is like to have the vapours and Maria might well change her mind about marrying me."

"If your rakehell ways do not daunt her, I doubt if Aunt Minerva's vapours will do so, but I shall delay the news a little longer if that is what you wish."

She smiled wanly as he went back into the drawing room. She remained in the hall staring at the closed door for an age. What she had hoped for so fervently had, after all, come to pass, but the result to herself was not at all what she still wished. However, despite her feelings she could not resent her father's happiness, nor Lady Moncourt's. Her warmth would be his salvation, and Jacey knew now her own portion was no longer encumbered, she could, herself, make a brilliant match. Only ...

Her wistful thoughts were interrupted by the arrival of a visitor. At a time of such poignant reflection Jacey felt she could not face any visitor with equanimity. Without waiting to be seen she turned on her heel but not before she heard the caller announce himself. The sound of his voice arrested her momentarily. The ache in her heart was an agonising torment and she remained only long enough to catch sight of Lord Sheringham being ushered towards the drawing room before she fled from the hall.

Pulling her shawl around her Jacey rushed out into the small garden at the rear of the house, and despite the coolness of the day she was determined to remain out there until the earl had gone. Speaking to him was more than she could bear, but she doubted if he would wish to see her in any event now. Even at that moment she calculated that Sir John would be informing him of the change in the situation. How relieved he would be to know he would be paid his debt without having to marry her.

She wandered disconsolately around the walled garden, wondering how long it would be before she could return to the house. Sheringham's interview with Sir John would not take long and accordingly she began to walk briskly back up the path towards the house. However, she had gone but a few steps when she saw him ahead of her. He was hatless and the cold breeze was ruffling his mass of dark curls. He stopped abruptly when he caught sight of her and although she automatically turned she knew there was nowhere to which she could go, and in any event if he wished to give her another set down before he took his leave it would at least be the final one. His gloating would not hurt her, for she could not find it in her heart to blame him his pleasure.

"The first time we met was in a garden," he said when he was close enough to be heard. "Do you recall it?"

"I could never forget," she answered truthfully, unable to meet his probing gaze.

Although his words mocked her, his manner, oddly enough, did not.

He smiled regretfully. "Indeed. You were so outraged, and with good cause."

"You are remarkable magnanimous, but, then, it is you who now has good cause."

She looked away and he went on, in a more brisk tone, "I have just this moment left Sir John and wished to speak with you before I go." He looked down at her slippered feet. "Miss Trevallion, are you not cold out here without your outdoor shoes and cloak?"

"Your concern is appreciated, Lord Sheringham, but I am often exposed to the elements at Trevallion Manor. I am immured to the cold, I assure you." She eyed him warily then. "I suppose Papa has apprised you of the news of his betrothal."

"I was delighted to wish him happy."

"You will also be relieved at being able to redeem your debt without recourse to more extreme measures."

He drew a small sigh. "Such circumstances would not have been conducive to a happy marriage, Miss Trevallion. We are both most fortunate to have averted a catastrophe."

She turned away again in order to hide her pain. "Then there is nothing more to say. I am persuaded you must be anxious to be away."

Her legs were so weak she was obliged to sit down on a rustic bench at the side of the path, hoping he would go away and leave her to her heartache. Unfortunately her self-control was fast deserting her. To her horror her shoulders began to shake with emotion and tears spilled on to her cheeks.

"Your own relief is more than evident," he told her, mistaking her emotion, which did nothing to stop her tears spilling over.

After a moment he handed her his lace-edged handkerchief and without a word Jacey took it from him. "I am making a cake of myself," she sobbed, desperately attempting to recover her composure. "I do beg your pardon, my lord."

"By no means. Your emotion is perfectly understandable to me. The gaining of a step-mother is not always welcome to a daughter who is accustomed to running her father's household."

"You are mistaken," she answered in a thick voice. "If I am to have a step-mother, Lady Moncourt is the most delightful."

"Then I would have thought you would be exhibiting more delight, gaining a step-mother you admire, and losing a prospective husband for whom you have no regard, and all in one day."

His words only served to make her sob the more. He sat down at her side, although she wished he would go away. She had no mind for him to witness her foolishness.

"We are both now mercifully free to follow our fancy," he said in a rallying tone which was quite at odds with her own feelings on the matter, although she did credit him with the attempt to cheer her.

"I have no doubt where yours will lead," she couldn't help retorting.

"I would wager that you are in error, Miss Trevallion. It might surprise you to learn that I have had a fancy for matrimony for some time past."

Jacey blew her nose on his handkerchief which was by now sodden. "Lady Sheringham will be relieved on both accounts. Whilst, no doubt, she wishes you wed, she will be pleased it is not to me."

His eyes opened wide in surprise. "What the devil makes you think so?"

She sniffed loudly, crushing the handkerchief in her fist. "It was quite obvious to me."

He turned to look at her tear-stained face, resting one arm along the back of the bench. "How odd you should think so. She told me I was more fortunate than I deserve." Jacey looked up at him at last to see him smile, "And I would be ... if you wanted to marry me."

"If?" She sat up straight. "But there is no longer any obligation. You have already expressed your relief in no uncertain terms," she added bitterly.

"It is to our mutual relief, I don't doubt. The fact remains that I would marry you now simply because I wished to. That is far better than any financial compulsion."

She stared at him in astonishment as he leaned forward and kissed her gently on the lips. The effect upon her was very much as it had been on that last occasion – devastating.

"I love you," he said as he drew away, "and have done ever since I saw you in Lord Dunscombe's Greek temple."

"You thought me one of Papa's lightskirts."

"I thought you were a goddess."

"You admitted to being foxed."

"I was, and that was because I had dreaded meeting you. In truth I expected Trevallion's daughter to be a hag-ridden spinster."

"And I thought you would be a monster!"

"Well, you can imagine my relief in discovering the goddess was actually my bride-to-be." He looked suddenly regretful. "What a pity you didn't feel as enchanted as I."

"Oh, I do now, my love," she cried. "Truly I do."

"That is all which matters," he answered, drawing her close to him again.

She went into his arms gladly, no longer resisting the wonder of his kisses which swept her to the heights of rapture. Her heart was unbelievingly light now that the burden of heartache had been lifted from it.

At the sound of approaching footsteps they drew apart a little. Breathless, Jacey exchanged a loving look with him when her aunt came hurrying towards them.

"Jacey! Jacey, dear, are you there? Oh, there you are." As he got to his feet, she said breathlessly, "Lord Sheringham, I had no notion you were here. I do beg your pardon." She sketched a curtsey and then addressed her niece once more. "Such a to-do. I suppose you have heard the news?"

"Is it not delightful, Aunt?"

Once again Jacey glanced at the earl, hardly daring to believe he actually loved her. It was all she could do not to pinch herself to make absolutely certain she was not dreaming.

"Yes, indeed, I would not dream of saying otherwise. Lady Moncourt is far too good for my brother, although that is her concern and I wish her joy of him, but how shall I bear up for two weddings in so short a time? They will not wait for long after you become leg-shackled."

Jacey laughed out of pure joy. "You will contrive, Aunt, never you fear."

"After it is all over you must come to Suffolk and stay with us for the summer," the earl invited. "The air will do wonders for your spirits, Miss Trevallion."

She flushed with pleasure. "How kind of you, Lord Sheringham. I only hope my niece is now more sensible of your worth."

He laughed, too, then. "I believe she is becoming a little more aware of it at last."

"And so she should! I fear this family has been a

sore trial to you."

"There have been moments when I considered myself fit for Bedlam, but I own the result is most satisfying."

Miss Trevallion cast him a curious look before addressing Jacey once more. "Your Papa, I fear, my dear, is a trifle bosky. Madame Fleur has arrived to fit your wedding gown, but Trevallion says you will not require it. What can he mean?"

Jacey exchanged a quick glance with the earl before answering, "No doubt he is foxed. Of couse I shall have my fitting. How else can my gown be made ready for me?"

Satisfied Miss Trevallion sketched a curtsey. "I shall go now and make haste tell her so before she obeys my brother's instructions."

"What instructions?" Jacey asked.

"Your father told her to take the gown and put in on his hack! She is so mortified she is like to do it, too."

As she hurried away down the path, Jacey laughed again before turning to Lord Sheringham. He took her hand in his drawing her close again.

"It would appear that I am not needed at present and I fear from now until the twenty-third we shall see little of each other. You will be surrounded by fussing females."

"Do not say so," she whispered in alarm, "for I want only to be with you."

He gazed at her lovingly. "I despaired of ever hearing you say so."

He bent his head and kissed her again. She clung to him, never wanting to leave the circle of his arms, but then he did release her. Taking her hand in his they began to walk back towards the house.

"After the twenty-third," he told her, "we'll be together every possible moment, for ever."

Jacey put her head against his shoulder, sighing with pleasure. It had all turned out so well after all.